INTO THE SILENT WORLD

Part Two of WHAT CAME AFTER

Sam Winston

unmediated ink™

ISBN: 0615918913
ISBN-13: 978-0615918914

Version 1.0

INTO THE SILENT WORLD

One:

Unlimited Resources

Hutchinson had been in charge of this platoon for the better part of six years, and until now they'd never gone door to door on anything other than a training mission. He didn't like it. There was bonus money to be had, plenty of it, but for once in his career no amount of bonus money seemed like enough. It wasn't that there was any particular danger involved. There wasn't really anything in the way of danger, come to that. You wouldn't find a weapon in a civilian's hand for twenty miles in any direction, and if you did it was some rusty old rabbit gun, unused now since there weren't any more rabbits to speak of. The rabbits all went when PharmAgra fixed the crops. Everything around here belonged to PharmAgra. These people were sharecroppers or less than sharecroppers. They weren't going to be taking a personal interest in much of anything Hutchinson and his Black Rose platoon set out to accomplish.

So even though the streets were weirdly empty and the doors were bolted shut everywhere and the wind whistled down the narrow alleyways like something ghostly from out of a past that didn't bear thinking about too closely, danger wasn't what had Hutchinson spooked.

What had him spooked was his own men. They were a little too eager. They were a lot too eager. He felt himself just on the feather edge of losing control, and he didn't like it.

Somebody was going to get shot. And unless that somebody was Henry Weller, it wasn't going to look especially good on Hutchinson's record.

*

How he figured it, the odds were long to begin with. No way on earth would Weller have been stupid enough to head back home after outrunning a Black Rose convoy and taking down the last goddamn Chinook helicopter in the fleet and wrecking Anderson Carmichael's precious BMW X9 on top of everything else. Hutchinson figured that that was probably the guy's worst offense, when you came down to it. Wrecking the fancy car that he was supposed to be handing over to the richest man in the world. The president of AmeriBank, no less. An individual with infinite resources to do you harm.

The damned car was worthless now, that was for sure. It had looked like crap from the air, according to the scouts who'd come in first. Not a smoking hulk like the Chinook but torn up beyond fixing. More a personal insult to Anderson Carmichael than anything. And word was that Carmichael didn't take insults all that well.

Which is where Black Rose came in. Hutchinson could imagine Bainbridge getting the call from Carmichael, tough old General Bainbridge who'd trained Weller on the rich man's behalf only to watch him go nuts and turn against the people who'd been so good to him. He could imagine Carmichael telling General Bainbridge that he wanted Weller taken care of and that money was no object, and he could imagine Bainbridge taking to that idea like a duck to water. After all, Weller was the one who'd blown up that irreplaceable Black Rose Chinook helicopter—which meant he was already at the top of Bainbridge's list. Having Carmichael offer to pick up the tab was pure gravy. You just couldn't beat capitalism, could you?

They'd pulled out everything they had. Once word came down that the Chinook was on the ground, the convoy set a new course for Farmington and forgot about that nowhere little X-marks-the-spot target in the middle of the tobacco fields. The radio brought the new orders in a series of sputtering bursts. Basically, they said *go door to door in Weller's home town and find that son of a bitch and bring him.* There would be double bonus money and certain credits toward promotion if he was breathing , but how much money did you need and how far up the ladder did you want to go? If the orders had specifically said *alive,* that would have been one thing. When they attached a bonus and promo credits to it, they were intentionally giving you some leeway. Such were the fine points of strategic military action, the understanding of which had put Hutchinson in charge of this platoon in the first place.

In addition to Weller himself, there were three secondary individuals called out in the orders. An Indian doctor, along with Weller's wife and child. The doctor they wanted alive—Hutchinson figured that was in case she had information that could be sold to the boys at PharmAgra—but the wife and child didn't have any such conditions attached. There weren't any delivery parameters connected to them at all. You were free to handle them however you might see fit. Hutchinson understood that perfectly well, too. It was another kind of leeway for another kind of strategic action. You could use them against Weller if you had the opportunity and the inclination. Hurt them a little. Hurt them a lot. Getting him to come along in the process. Getting him to maybe start seeing the world from your perspective for a change.

Call Hutchinson old fashioned, call him soft-hearted, but that wasn't a strategy that appealed to him. Other platoon leaders—other individual soldiers, come to that—would understand it differently. Where he saw fruitless harm and maybe even moral turpitude if there was anything like moral turpitude left in the world, they'd just see an angle. So he told his platoon *hands off the women.* He was within his rights to make that call. It was the burden of command. A lot of reflexive bellyaching came back to him as a result, a lot of moaning and a lot of groaning and a lot of the usual frustrated *aww Lieutenant* bullshit, but you had to expect that kind of thing. Everybody was charged up. Every man was on edge. It was the platoon leader's duty to keep them there, without letting them go over.

*

His platoon was the last of three in. That made a whole company going house to house in pursuit of one individual, knocking down doors and terrorizing civilians. Sometimes there weren't even doors to knock down. Just tarps hanging. A hundred and fifty men pushing those tarps aside with the barrels of their automatic weapons, hardware that must have looked to these ignorant filthy cowering people like some kind of technology sent down from outer space.

He'd never seen such poverty, such misery. He thought he'd seen it when he'd left home and run off to sign up with Black Rose all those years back, back when the Great Dying had taken away pretty much everything he'd had in the way of a family, but those conditions were starting to look pretty good compared to right here. That's what happened when you spent all your time closeted away in DC. You didn't get out and breathe. You didn't see the world. You didn't know how completely things had fallen off a cliff out here in the Zone.

His men came at these people like creatures from a different race of beings altogether. Something that had grown up bigger and stronger than old style human beings, and far more aggressive as a result. Two or three steps up the food chain, by the look of it. He kept an eye on their progress from the street, smoking a cigar in the driver's seat of an open Humvee with the engine idling, wondering which way evolution had worked in this case. Maybe both ways. Up and down. Forward and backward. These people were falling apart in ways that Hutchinson didn't recognize from his own childhood. They looked tough and wasted at the same time. Worn out from work but not worn out enough to quit working. That was probably how PharmAgra wanted it.

His men were moving in twos and threes. His second-in-command was Bates. Sergeant Bates, just now emerging from underneath a blue tarp behind a specialist named Parker. Parker looked frustrated and Bates looked pissed off. It was early evening and the temperature was still high and there wasn't any air moving. Those little hovels and falling-in apartments must have been ovens. He didn't know how people could live there. No wonder they didn't mind working their asses off in the PharmAgra fields. Why stay home even if you could?

The men kept on. Hutchinson put the Humvee in gear and moved up into the lead. A dozen units came along behind him in formation, keeping pace, strung out like bulbs on a wire. He stopped at a streetcorner that was mostly wasteland on all four sides. The buildings thinned out here, and the parking lots between them held little stands of brush that had drifted in and recovered the space for something like nature. Scrubby trees and dry grasses. The kind of plants that would grow anywhere but didn't do you any good because they didn't provide food or shade or anything else that you could use. The kind of worthless overgrowth that would take over the world when people were done using it.

He missed DC. He missed good old White Washington, the pale public city of high domes and marble columns, the place that Black Rose had claimed for its own in the same way that AmeriBank had claimed New York and National Motors had claimed Detroit and Family Health Partnership had claimed Chicago. Parts of Washington looked like this—the old abandoned residential and commercial districts—but nobody lived there. Hutchinson turned around in his seat and drew on his cigar and watched the platoon work its way toward him. Crackling sounds and bits of angry voices coming over the radio like the sounds of frustration itself made physical and turned loose. No progress beyond movement. Sometimes that's the way it went. You tried to educate the men about it, but you weren't always successful.

One building at this ruined corner caught his eye. The pavement in front of it was grassed over in spots, but not as thoroughly as elsewhere. There was no brush and there were no trees. Nature hadn't gotten as much of a foothold here. Someone had worked at holding it off, at least until recently.

He guessed he knew who.

Set back into the lot past the paving was a low-slung garage building painted white a long time ago. Gone mostly back to raw cinder blocks now, since nobody could get any paint. The garage had a single roll-up door that was rolled down, and across the wide lintel above it you could still read the script, *"Mechanic On Duty!"*

That would be Henry Weller.

No wonder the place looked decently kept up. Weller didn't work for PharmAgra. He ran a repair shop that fixed things for money and Ameri-Bank scrip and whatever else anybody had to give him, so this would be both his home and his place of business. Under normal circumstances he'd spend all day here. Hutchinson got out of the Humvee to do a little recon. He didn't think he'd find anything. He didn't think Weller would ever set foot on this property again, never mind right this minute when he had to know Black Rose was after him.

He rolled up the overhead door and went into the garage, past the most hopeless and patched-together collection of tools you ever saw. It looked like a blacksmith shop out of that Longfellow. It looked like something dug up from the Bronze Age. There was a Franklin stove standing in the middle with a gas line running to it. That was really something, provided it worked. Hutchinson followed the line and opened the valve and sure enough. Gas. Nobody had gas around here. God knows where Weller got it.

Behind the garage was a house that wasn't anything special unless you considered the alternatives. It was clean, for one thing, with a kitchen you walked into first and a living room behind that and then two bedrooms. An ancient toilet in the bathroom. He took a leak and lifted the handle and stood watching the water swirl away down the drain to God knows where, feeling like royalty. The tank filled right back up again with water that must have been stored someplace Hutchinson hadn't seen. Imagine that. This place was turning out to be the Taj Mahal. It was turning out to remind Hutchinson of the place where he'd grown up, until he'd run off and finished coming of age under the supervision of Black Rose.

A crackling over the radio got him moving. Bates shouting orders to pull back, pull back. The sound of his voice breaking down under static. Hutchinson checked his fly and ducked out of the bathroom and through the house and back into the garage. Scrambling out onto the concrete lot. The Humvee sat there in the gathering dark as if he'd just stopped for gas, or as if somebody'd set it up as part of a diorama showing the old days when anybody might stop for gas. When there was gas to be had and people could afford to buy it. When people had someplace to go.

He ran past the Humvee and into the street, looking back to where the city was beginning to erupt in flames. It had happened fast, and it was still happening. Either someone had thrown an incendiary grenade or someone had used a flame thrower, although it could have been both. Both at the same time or one after the other. Once these things started they didn't like to stop. Doorways and open windows sprouted flame. Brittle old wooden buildings with tarpaper roofs were going up like kindling, and the pathetic jumbled goods inside them—ruined furniture, strewn bales of pilfered straw that whole families slept on like so many animals, sad collections of hand-me-downs from a world that was long gone and never coming back—went up fast too. There were already people lying dead or dying on the sidewalk and more people were emerging from doorways now to stumble over them. These new arrivals falling themselves. Some of them on fire, drifting helplessly to the ground among or upon their friends and neighbors and loved ones, nothing but human ashes and human smoke. No one responsible. No one you could single out.

Hutchinson's men had fallen back at Bates's order. They were gathered at the assigned location, a crossroads a few dozen yards this side of where the worst of it had started, shouldering one another in a tight circle on the cracked pavement. Just watching things fall around them. The smoke made some of them cough, bringing to their eyes the only tears that they would shed. A black form crawled toward them wailing, smoke curling up behind it, and someone put it out of its misery. Hutchinson didn't see who. A murmur went through the men as he approached, a kind of low pleading that rose up louder and became one voice asking him could they finish the job now.

Automatic gunfire from down the block. The ferocious sound of one of the other platoons at work.

He didn't know how he'd stop them, so he gave the order. All he could think of was that PharmAgra wasn't going to like this one little bit. A big chunk of their labor force, lost for no reason. A big chunk of their customer base, too. It was going to cost them a pretty penny, which meant they'd put the screws to Bainbridge at Black Rose. Which was bad news for everyone.

Two:

What Came Next

They were making themselves into pack animals. A mule train without mules. A wagon train without wagons. Just a dozen refugee families shouldering as much as they could of the little bit they'd accumulated in this life—which wasn't much but was nonetheless more than they could carry.

"If you're not sure you can haul it all the way," said Weller, "then don't bring it. We don't want to leave a trail."

By *all the way*, he meant all the way from Connecticut to South Carolina. From the Northeastern Empowerment Zone to a wilderness that wasn't zoned at all. A journey like that would take the better part of a month on foot even under the best of circumstances, and these circumstances were a lot less than promising. It would be a pioneering effort. They would almost surely lose people, although he made no mention of that. Just as long as they didn't lose his wife or his daughter. Weller believed that he could reconcile himself to almost anything, as long as he could hang on to Liz and Penny.

They'd already lost the schoolteacher. His body lay where they'd left it, covered as decently as circumstances would permit, under a linen sheet among the trampled tobacco plants. Just another shapeless bundle in a landscape pocked with baggage. If the schoolteacher had people, a family or even close friends, it didn't show. Everyone had been more or less ignoring his body for the last panicked and raw-nerved hour. Then again, try naming a single one of them who wasn't in shock. The Black Rose helicopter that had gone down in a fireball of its own napalm was burning and burning off to the north, a sluggish plume of greasy black smoke rising into the day like a marker. The air smelled like a hundred kinds of death.

Weller found a shovel and dug a hole near the perimeter of the field and buried the schoolteacher's body. Everybody else was occupied. Nobody else seemed to have thought of doing it. Perhaps it was just too much to bear.

He didn't pray over the grave. Nobody prayed anymore. He tamped the dirt down and went back to the gathering of low-roofed dugout huts. He thought about whether or not he ought to bring the shovel south with everything else they were hauling. He assessed the weight of it and tested its balance over his shoulder. Above all he asked himself if he had ever needed a shovel on that last trip he'd taken—the first time he'd traveled to Spartanburg, fending for himself and nursing that Army motorcycle along until it got wrecked in what had turned out to be Greensboro—and the truth was that he couldn't remember ever thinking *if I only had a shovel, things would be better*. That settled it. He jammed the blade deep into the hard dirt of the tobacco field and walked away. You couldn't take everything. He'd said that himself. You had to be ruthless.

Food and clothing. Patel's precious collection of seeds and samples and cuttings, damp inside their glassine envelopes and burlap sacks. Such quantities of disengineered tobacco as they'd already harvested and dried and packed up for the black market. Those things you brought, no question. Plus anything irreplaceable that didn't weigh too much. There was stuff in this world that you could never get your hands on again. One of a kind objects or objects so rare that they might as well be. Things that this whole outpost full of people had worked like galley slaves to obtain through a vague network of black markets and criminal runners. A microscope, for example, and a couple of test probes that ran on electricity you couldn't be sure of getting anywhere but just might. There were the bigger and heavier things they'd built by hand, too. Power converters and generators. Ideas made real.

That was the stuff that made you think twice.

"We can't leave the generator behind," said Patel. Doctor Patel, the matriarch of this ruined place.

"I wouldn't be so sure," said Weller. "Anything you've built—anything *we've* built—" making that small adjustment either to indicate the work he'd done around here before or to show that he was ready to do it all once again—"we can always build again."

She turned and looked down into the hole where she'd lived for who knows how long, the expression on her face as desolate as the place she was leaving behind. She looked just about ready to break down, until he took her by the elbow. Offering just enough human contact to make a difference.

"Here," he said. "Let Janey help you decide what we can leave. It's OK. Honest. Let this be one thing you don't have to be in charge of, all right?"

Janey was midway between his daughter's age and his own, brand new to this great big world but tough-minded and a quick study and good with her hands. The lost pride of Spartanburg, gone off with a stranger to see the real world and now headed back. He waved her over and she came at a trot. By God she looked like a child compared to Patel. Patel was old enough, but she looked ancient now. As if nearly all of the life left in her had been drained out by the fury of that Black Rose assault. He wondered how she'd endure another run-in with them, to say nothing of the month-long trip to Spartanburg.

He'd been figuring they'd lose people. He hoped she wouldn't be one of them.

He went back and got the shovel.

*

Travel was slow that first day. They'd find a better rhythm as time went by, Weller was sure of it, but when you had a handful of little kids to keep tabs on and one old woman with a broken spirit you couldn't expect much. It was inch by inch. Nobody had spoken as they cut their trail southward, staying off the roads and in such forested areas as they could find. Moving like deer, copse to copse. Always in the shadow of something. Until here it was sundown and they'd gone he didn't dare calculate how far. Not very. The plume of smoke from the big burning Chinook helicopter was still visible in the distance, merging into the dusk and sagging with the humidity of the night air. It felt to Weller as if they'd covered no ground at all.

They hadn't seen any more Black Rose, though. They certainly hadn't seen the convoy that Weller and Janey had outrun just the day before. No more helicopters either. That was good news, if you wanted to look at it that way. Perhaps they weren't being pursued after all. Perhaps Black Rose had decided that their mission was accomplished. Then again, perhaps not.

Either way, they settled in for the night rather than keep moving. A party as big as theirs couldn't stay in motion after dark. They could hardly stay in motion at all, but that was a different problem altogether. You could press on through that. You could urge people forward. You could motivate them and persuade them and manage to keep going one way or another. Darkness, on the other hand, was impassible.

They dared not light a fire. The woods encroached on their camp, soundless except for the movement of a little wind in the treetops. Low clouds hid the stars, and everything was black. Children, boys and girls who'd never known anything but the peaceful little village outpost where they'd spent the entirety of their short lives, innocent youngsters grown accustomed to quiet evenings by the warm and cheerful fireside, clung to their parents and peered out into the darkness and tried not to be afraid.

All but one. Little Penny, Weller's five-year-old daughter, was up and about and pretty much everywhere at once. Her mother could hardly keep track of her. It seemed to Penny that she could see in the dark, and although that probably wasn't true it was true enough. After everything she'd been through—after the slow endless years of going blind, and after the difficult and singular restoration of her sight in that New York hospital—she wanted to see everything and she believed that she could. Nothing in the world was beyond possible.

The adults gathered together in a wide circle, seated on fallen logs and mossy rocks, whispering to one another in the dark. No bugs chittered and no birds whistled and no mice rattled through the dry underbrush. Nothing lived except the greenblack forest itself and these unwilling travelers pausing in it. They were accustomed to the silence, but they didn't like it. Most of them, Patel in particular, had spent the better parts of their lives waging battle against the silent world they'd inherited when PharmAgra eradicated the insects and starved the birds and drove the mice to extinction or the next worst thing,

Henry Weller wasn't accustomed to holding forth, but he held forth now. "It's all different in Spartanburg," he said. "They've got plants that haven't been raised anywhere else in fifty years."

"I've heard stories," came a man's voice from the dark. "I've always taken it for wishful thinking." It was clear from his tone that he still did. "We don't have time to chase fairy tales."

"It's no fairy tale," said Weller. "I've been there. I just got back. And Janey, here—Spartanburg is where she grew up."

"It was paradise," Janey put in.

"I wouldn't go that far."

"It was paradise for food, then."

"I'll grant you that," said Weller. "They've got watermelon and sweet corn and a dozen kinds of tomatoes you've never even heard about. They've got cattle for food and cattle for milk. They've got bugs pollinating everything and birds eating the bugs."

A couple of jaws dropped open. He could see them by what little moonlight had begun to filter down through the cloud cover. It was amazing how much you could see in the dark, really—how little the human body could accustom itself to in the way of input, and how much it could make of what thin scraps you gave it.

"That's right," he said. "Birds. They've come back, or else maybe they never left to begin with. You ought to see them. You *will* see them." A sigh passed around the circle. Even the children took notice, turning their heads away from the treacherous depths of the woods to look his way instead. Weller stored the promise of birds away right then, knowing instinctively that just the mention of a flock of blue jays or whatever would be sufficient to get at least part of this crowd through one of the difficult stretches sure to lie ahead.

"If it's really such a paradise," Patel said, "and I'm not saying isn't, then maybe they won't want us sticking our noses where they don't belong."

"You've got a point," said Weller. He pulled on his lip and thought out loud, explaining that the secret of Spartanburg's success was its utter removal from the rest of the corrupted world. The whole place was a sealed environment, or it had been until he'd come along. Nobody got in or out. Nobody inside even knew there was a habitable world outside.

Janey said he was right about that. Here she was twenty-some years old, and until a week or so ago she'd thought Spartanburg was the only place on earth where people could manage to live.

The amazed shaking of heads all around.

She said she knew now that it was a trick. A plot on the part of a couple of old Black Rose mercenaries who'd run off into seclusion when the Great Dying had hit so long ago. Taking with them a couple of hundred likely followers and occupying the old car factory outside of town and sealing it up tight against whatever was becoming of the planet and the human race and everything. Then the lies began. The lies about what was happening outside. The head of the operation—Colonel Marlowe—went out beyond the walls on recon from time to time, she said.

"Except he didn't," Weller put in. "Not really."

No. He didn't go anywhere. He told everybody that he went out, but he didn't really. All he did, Janey explained, was stay in his quarters and cook up stories. Stories about disease and desolation, about viruses that turned people into ravenous things that couldn't die and wanted to. About death in a thousand forms you couldn't even imagine.

Weller said that everybody in Spartanburg thought Marlowe and his second in command, Major Oates, were heroes, when the truth was that they weren't much better than jailers. Two old men hanging onto power they'd grabbed when the grabbing was good.

She disagreed, if only a little. She said even Weller had to admit that things in Spartanburg were pretty good as long as you didn't know you were being held against your will. The food was terrific and there was work to do and everything was peaceful, as opposed to the way things had gone out here. Out here things had gone to hell. In Spartanburg it was paradise. You had to expect to meet some kind of God in paradise.

"I guess so," said Weller. "Even if he's just a little bitty one, made out of tin."

*

13

In the middle of the night, with everyone asleep under burlap sacks spread out on the raw ground, a pair of helicopters passed over. They came in low, barely skimming the treetops, swooping and darting like venomous insects with searchlights depending from their bellies like slung weapons. Hard beams of white light strafed the greenery but failed, in the end, to penetrate it.

*

"There's another thing," Weller said to Patel as they ate a cold breakfast. "Black Rose? The best equipped killers in the world? The bunch that shot your schoolteacher and torched your fields and would have murdered the whole lot of you if we hadn't run? They're scared to death of Spartanburg. They won't go near the place."

"I don't understand."

"They've built up this picture of it in their minds. The fellow who runs Black Rose and the fellow behind Spartanburg—that Colonel Marlowe—they used to be rivals in the Navy. They were a couple of SEALS who went their separate ways when push came to shove, and they've hated each other ever since. Plus, Spartanburg put up a good defense from the start. They took down one or two Black Rose choppers that got close—no missiles or anything, strictly radio intercept stuff—and Black Rose got gun-shy. They've left Spartanburg alone ever since. Man, oh, man. The stories I heard before I went down there. You'd have thought it was the end of the world, instead of the beginning."

"There are other places we could go, though. Closer places. Other stations where people do work like mine."

"Where?" Folks in the traveling party were stretching, gathering up their belongings, fixing to get started. Weller motioned to Penny and she came near and he tossed her his battered Black Rose compass. She studied it as if it were a relic recovered from some vanished civilization, which after all it surely was. "Give that to your mom," he said. "We'll be westbound today. You two are in charge." And then, turning back to Patel, "Do you know how we'd go about getting to one of those other stations?"

"Not offhand," she said. "But there are runners, Henry. There are people out here who'd know."

"We can't wait around for them to show up. And we can't go looking. Not with this crowd depending on us."

"These people will never survive a trip like the one you have in mind."

"Maybe not all of them," he said, "but those who do will have it made. And so will you."

Patel lifted her pack onto her shoulders, looking more than a little shellshocked. She didn't know what to think of Henry Weller. She thought he'd changed—not that she'd known him all that completely before. He'd been a different person when their paths had crossed the first time, though, when his mission to recover Penny's eyesight had led him to her little outpost in the tobacco fields of Connecticut. The tainted earth produced genetically modified tobacco everywhere in what remained of the state except right there, right there in that little patch of ground sequestered off by repurposed PharmAgra fencelines, right there in that secret acreage where Patel and her people had disengineered the stuff back to its natural and strictly forbidden state. All that Weller had wanted to do then was lend a hand. He hadn't wanted to run things, and he certainly hadn't wanted to make important decisions as if they were his to make.

Back then—not so long ago, really; just a month or two although it seemed like forever—back then he was just the father of a little girl, traveling on nerve and devotion into a world whose terrors he couldn't begin to predict. He'd been good with his hands and he'd been kind enough to spend a couple of weeks upgrading the station's infrastructure, and she had to admit that there had been more than a few moments when she'd hoped he might decide to stick around forever. Go back to Farmington for his wife, abandon the crazy idea of finding a cure for his daughter, and just settle in where he could do some real good. But she had underestimated him. Everyone had underestimated him—everyone including Black Rose and PharmAgra and the people from AmeriBank to whom nothing mattered but money—because apparently not one of them had considered for a moment that he might accomplish what he'd set out to accomplish.

And yet he had. And the doing of it had either changed him or re-vealed him, it was hard to say which. Regardless, she couldn't just yield eve-rything.

She fixed him with a hard look. "We'd still have a home, you know, if not for you." She knew that the accusation wasn't entirely fair, and she cer-tainly knew that it was cruel, but she said it anyway. "We'd still be moving the work forward. Our schoolteacher—he had a name, you know, and he had parents of his own up near Hartford somewhere, and he had his whole life ahead of him—would still be among the living."

"I know all that. Don't think for a minute that I don't."

"But now you want to be in charge."

"No. Now *you need me* to be in charge."

"You act like you've earned it."

"I'm not acting like anything. I'm just being practical."

A line was forming up. Families grouped together and fathers with children on their backs in addition to the perilous burdens of food and es-sentials they carried. Weller sized them up and thought he knew about how long that setup would last. Within an hour or so the children would be walking and the whole column would be moving at the pace of its slowest member.

Patel watched too. "Even if we do get to Spartanburg," she said, "what do you suppose will happen? What if they don't want us in paradise? How will we even get inside?"

"We'll get inside all right," Weller said. "When Janey and I took off, we left the back door wide open."

Three:

Dawn

The children were all born within these walls. Call it a fortress or call it a prison, call it some combination of both, they'd never called it anything at all. They didn't need a word for it, because to them it was the whole world.

What natural light there was came sifting down through windows so high as to be accessible only to birds. Dawn came late and night came early, in the cruel and implacable way that time and daylight move among high mountains. The children went off to school in the same dark every day, down the paved lane that passed for a street in their roofed-over neighborhood. The lamps would still be on, corner by corner, and the children would come to the edge of the lined-up houses and enter into the sector of dim shops and shuttered workrooms where their parents would spend the day to come. Thus would they pass their own intractable futures, for this was all the world that the world held.

Beyond the walls was nothing. It was a place of nightmares, nameless because giving names to nightmares only invites them in. It was a place where everything that could die had already died, and a place where the insatiable things that could not die lived on and on and on.

*

But on this singular morning the children saw a new light up ahead. A light that didn't spill down from high above but instead came creeping at a low

17

angle, earthbound and strange, leaking in from somewhere out past the ballfield and the weedy concrete lots where ranks of old cars waited for delivery to a world that didn't exist anymore.

The children were drawn to the light. Who wouldn't be? It illuminated things that had never been illuminated before, at least not in the memory of man. The undersides of soaring girders. Dusty corners and low passageways. Motes of dust like clouds. It entered like some threat or some promise, like some new reality asserting itself, and the children were too innocent to know which of these it might be.

Their parents would have run the other way. They would have pulled the alarms and called out the militia, and under the command of Major Oates their world would have been returned to normal. Anything that had entered with that bloom of light would have been hunted down and destroyed. After all, that was what the militia was for. That was the promise of Major Oates himself. Nothing less than the maintenance of the world.

But the children didn't run. They didn't pull the alarms. Perhaps they couldn't reach. Perhaps they were too distracted. Apparently no one had thought of that. No one had imagined that everything would depend on a handful of little children making their way to school in the interrupted dark.

Instead of hesitating, they drew near. One at a time and then more. A handful of them. A half circle. They spoke not so much as a word, gathering together inside the fallen overhead door with the sunlight blazing through to sever the darkness and illuminate their small faces. They stood that way for a long time, until one among them stepped out into the brilliant and welcoming day. Which caused the world to erupt into something entirely new.

Four:

Tracks

They were in a no-man's land somewhere deep in the Northeastern Empowerment Zone, out in some nameless place that people had abandoned long ago for places that turned out to be no better after all and maybe even worse, and still they inched westward. They'd scrambled over some long bridge in the dark, a bridge that arched what had to be the Hudson. They were lucky to have found a crossing at all, lucky that they hadn't come upon the river a half-mile to the north or south and missed it altogether. The water had moved silently beneath their feet as they made the crossing on ruined and treacherous pavement, black water intermittently visible by starlight and moonlight. No one had had to say *watch your footing.* You watched your footing with every step you took in this treacherous world. They'd waited until dark for the concealment it gave and then gone on across, moving in a tight line and keeping low, slipping from stanchion to stanchion and concealing themselves as if there were eyes everywhere in the surrounding wasteland.

Only once they'd gotten past the bridge did they stop to rest.

Apple orchards. Or what looked like apple orchards. There weren't any apples. Everything was dead, the crabbed branches like grasping hands reaching up to claw at the stars. Weller asked Patel and she said yes, these were apple trees all right. New York used to have plenty of them.

Once upon a time the ground here beneath the trees would have been rich and damp with rotting fruit. It was barren now, hard dry dirt beneath

19

hard low leafless trees, and they sat hungry with their backs against the trunks. They'd taken from home what food they could, but it would never be enough. Rations were short.

You couldn't just eat anything you found out here, either, provided you were lucky enough to find something to begin with. In an ironic way that meant thank God the apple trees were dead, because who could have resisted their fruit? Which of these hungry individuals could have kept himself from reaching up into their branches and pulling down a rich round Rome or McIntosh or Northern Spy? And which of them would have not been poisoned as a result, either right away or long-term, by the changes that the chemists and geneticists and marketing geniuses at PharmAgra had made so long ago to everything edible that grew? The modifications they'd made to the apples—to make them bigger, sweeter, and crisper, faster to ripen and easier to ship—were no doubt the same modifications that had killed the trees in the end. An unintended consequence, but just as well for this little band of travelers who'd come to rest beneath their branches. They shared around a loaf of bread made from wheat purchased months ago on the black market—there weren't too many loaves left, and before long they'd have to take their chances and throw themselves upon the mercy of any such wild plants as might have remained unmodified back before the Great Dying, weeds and pine nuts and wild berries and so forth—they shared bread and one or two of them remembered their Old Testament lessons and felt like the Hebrews of old, cast out into the desert with no time to have made any preparations at all.

They leaned their heads back and looked skyward into the starlight, up through the scrabbling of the twisted trees, and they yearned for some kind of solace. Only Dr. Patel, the oldest of them all and probably the only one who remembered real untainted apples—certainly the only one who had worked for PharmAgra during the years when science was taking things apart and putting them back together in forms that were worth more money—only Patel looked not at the stars but at the tangled branches that scratched their dead fingers toward them. Toward the magnetism of them and the magnetism of other worlds. And only she, among them all, wept freely for the loss of everything.

*

Weller leaned up against a tree and Liz leaned up against the same tree right alongside him. The tree wasn't very big around and the two of them were like twelve and three on the face of a clock. Penny snuggled in between them and went to sleep. They wanted to do the same but couldn't, no matter what.

Liz sighed. "For a while, I kept thinking we could just go home."

"When'd you give up on that idea?"

"About when the whole army started coming after us." She smiled into the dark for his benefit, as if there were anything humorous about it.

"Maybe one day," Weller said.

They sat for a while in the darkness under the trees, listening to Penny breathing softly in her sleep. It took a child to sleep under these conditions. It took innocence.

Liz asked, "Are you sure about Spartanburg?"

"What's not to be sure about?"

She took her time answering. "It's a long trip, is all. It's a long way from home."

"I know. But right now it's a much better place to be—especially for Penny. She'll be safe there. We can pull ourselves together. Get our footing back."

"We've never had all that much in the way of footing."

He reached across the child and took his wife's hand. "I know that, too."

"But we've always gotten by."

Penny's body twitched in her sleep. One leg shot out as if it had been touched with an electric current, jolting straight into the dark and quivering there. After a few seconds she grew calmer and whimpered once and lay still again.

"She's exhausted," her father said.

Her mother sighed. "Me too. And we've got such a long way to go."

"It'll get better."

"I don't want things to get better. I want things the way they used to be."

"The way they used to be, our little girl was almost blind." But even though it was true, he didn't entirely mean it. He didn't entirely mean it because he knew that it wasn't what Liz was talking about and he knew that saying it would hurt her, would throw up a wall between them, which it did. He was sorry before he'd even finished saying it.

"And *you* saved her," she said. "I didn't want you to go but you went anyhow, and you proved me wrong, and you saved her."

"Liz—"

"I spent a month with her in the hospital, too."

"I know you did—"

That could have been the extent of it, but it wasn't. Once these things got started, they were hard to stop. Even now. Even under these circumstances. Especially under these circumstances. If they were to be stopped, someone had to want to stop them.

She drew breath. "In the process," she said, "you put all these lives at risk. You got that poor teacher killed. You could have gotten us all killed, for that matter."

"Lucky us." Trying to put a little spin on it.

"It's your fault."

"Not all of it."

"You set it in motion."

"That I did."

Another moment went by, filled up with nothing but night.

"But it was for a good cause," he said. "You have to admit that."

She didn't answer.

"You have to admit it."

Still nothing.

"Are you saying—"

"I'm not saying anything."

"You're not saying you'd swap her vision for going back to the way things were?"

"I'm tired, Henry. I'm very tired."

"I know. I'm tired too."

In between them, Penny jumped again.

*

She woke up shivering. The morning wasn't particularly cold and the ground beneath the trees was mostly dry and her parents had pressed themselves against her from either side when they'd finally gone to sleep themselves, so it wasn't the temperature. And she wasn't sick. Her mother pressed a hand against her forehead and followed it with a long kiss of assessment, but the child's temperature was normal. She wasn't feverish. What she was was disoriented. Nervous. Shaken up and shaking, distressed for no reason she could put words to. Like a person just let into prison, or one just let out.

Her mother hugged her close, because what else was there to do?

Around them, people were rising up. Bodies shifting and low voices murmuring and people clearing the night from their throats.

Liz asked her daughter what it was, what was the matter.

Penny said nothing for the longest time. She just pressed herself against her mother, as if her mother's body could absorb the woe that had overcome her. Liz holding her tight with the very same impulse, the impulse of all parents everywhere, the irrational and hopeless belief that you can remove your child's troubles by taking them upon yourself.

The two of them together, then, mother and child, against the rough tree and upon the rough ground and with the father looking on helpless. The rest of the traveling party was coming slowly to their feet, bent beneath the lowest branches and moving outward. Soon they were all up and moving around but Weller's little family, all of them looking their way with curiosity or question or even anxiety, for who would lead them on if not Weller? Their allegiance had not shifted away from Dr. Patel, but it had allowed itself a detour. Yet they all remained distant, respectful of Weller and the child and the mother, making a kind of charmed circle among the trees. Waiting.

Liz relaxed her hold just the slightest, indicating that perhaps something might have changed or be about to, but Penny didn't take the opportunity to pull away. She only sighed and stiffened and shivered more, pressing in, hiding within her mother's embrace from who knows what. From everything.

Janey broke the circle at last. She stepped across a weedy gap in between the trees and bend over to enter into the space that the Wellers had claimed for their own. From such claims or seeming claims whole cities grow, but not here. Not now. She looked from Penny to her father and asked him, "What gives? What's with the kid?" Just as plainly as that. *The kid.* As if she and Weller had a charmed circle of their own, into which his wife and daughter had intruded.

Liz looked hard at her. Weller didn't look at her at all. Penny tilted her head back and looked upward from beneath the twisted limbs and her eyes rolled back in her head and she whispered, "It's on fire."

*

That was the end of it. The words came out of her and she grew relaxed and calm. She stretched and stood to her feet between her mother's outstretched legs, blinking her eyes and asking what was for breakfast.

"The usual," said Janey. "I'll go." She ducked away toward where Patel sat on a fallen trunk, pulling chunks from a loaf of bread and passing them out one by one.

"Don't do *the kid* any favors," said Liz. Mostly to herself and a little to her husband and not really to Janey at all.

Weller turned to Penny. "What did you mean, *it's on fire?*"

"Shh," said Liz. "Not now."

"Not now? Then when?"

"Later. Now isn't the time."

Penny wasn't listening. She was busy watching Janey collect their breakfast.

"It's fresh in her mind now."

"It was a dream, Henry. It didn't mean anything. She didn't mean anything by saying it." Sitting there with her back to the tree and watching her daughter. Missing the feel and the smell and the weight of her. "It was just words."

Weller shook his head.

Somebody went scouting and found a creek and brought back water to supplement the supply they'd been carrying. A couple of buckets full. People were drinking from cupped hands and splashing it onto their faces and wishing out loud that they could heat some up to wash up with, but you didn't dare light a fire. It had been a couple of days since those helicopters had passed over, but you couldn't drop your guard. They'd had fires back home in the tobacco field, fires in their underground dugouts to cook over and to keep warm, and even a couple of gas stoves once Weller had hooked them up to the methane that they hadn't even known was generating itself under the dump a half-mile distant, but the world was a known place then. Now you couldn't be sure of anything. They missed home and they missed the tobacco fields and they missed that raw methane that came obligingly up from the ground to cook dinner with. It all seemed remote and impossible and miraculous now, vanished into the unrecoverable past.

Weller dug in his pack for a bit of plastic sheeting and set it inside the crown of his baseball cap, making a bowl. He held the hat out by the brim and touched Penny with it. "Why don't you go get us all a drink of water," he said, and she was happy to do her part. She ran out with the ball cap in her hand and the wind of her movement blew the plastic sheeting free and she had to chase it along the row of apple trees, laughing. Completely recovered, by the look of her. Her father watched her go, watched her stop and collect the sheeting and arrange it back inside his hat, watched her light out again toward the man with the buckets, thinking all the while that maybe Liz was right. Maybe it was just a dream after all.

"I'm sorry we had some hard words last night," he said as they watched her line up for water. Penny was bouncing on her toes, happy among the other children. It did his heart good. "You're not alone in thinking that I'm the one who fouled everything up."

"Henry. That's not what I meant."

"Then what."

"I just meant there are consequences, that's all. Consequences to everything."

"You're telling me."

She didn't answer.

"You're telling me, when I know better than anybody. You're putting us right back where we were before, Liz. You didn't want me to risk taking her to New York, but I did it and now I'm paying the price."

"You're not."

"I am."

"I didn't mean it that way."

"It's a different price. But I'm still paying."

At the front of the line Penny held out the ball cap with both of her hands, and the man with the bucket tipped as much water into it as she could manage. Maybe a little more. She turned slowly and came teetering back toward her mother and father, walking like a girl on a tightrope.

"I want to get home as much as you do," he said. "Every bit."

Janey arrived with half a loaf of bread just as Penny arrived with the precarious ball cap, and she tossed it to Weller who caught it one-handed. Liz looking over as if they'd just traded some coded message. Weller noting the look and tossing the bread on to her, conceding to Liz the right to parcel out such things among them. By her stance Janey had seemed about to sit down, to take a moment's rest under the tree, but at the last moment she thought better of it and kept moving. Not as if she meant to be unsociable, but as if she had other things to do before they got under way, which was surely the case.

*

Tracks in the sky and tracks on the ground. A few days had gone by without anything, just the group of them moving across the landscape in a slow line making slow progress, and now this. A contrail overhead from east to west, high enough that you couldn't see the plane that was making it. You couldn't hear it either. One of the children saw it first and his arm went up pointing and then everyone saw it. The whole line of march freezing in place instantly, twenty-five or thirty people going stiff as so many field mice caught beneath the gaze of an eagle. The irony of such a thing passing unnoticed in a world where there weren't eagles anymore and there weren't field mice either, a poisoned world where predation had taken entirely different forms.

Most of them had seen a few contrails before, and those sightings had been the closest they'd come to any aircraft whatsoever before the Black Rose helicopters had shown up. Back in those innocent days, machines that could fly had seemed far off and utterly irrelevant, visions or manifestations from some other world. Not any more. Now they were threats.

They waited for a while, keeping still, but they couldn't keep still forever. Weller shouted back down the line that they had to get going one of these days, and when nobody moved Dr. Patel shouted down the line that they weren't the only people out here after all, were they? There were runners. There were other settlements or rumors of them. What the men in the plane had seen if they'd seen anything at all—if they were even looking, or if they could detect anything whatsoever from such a height—might have been anyone. Her opinion made sense. And enough of the party listened to make a difference, so they grumbled and started forward again across the trackless tall grass, one by one and two by two, sluggish as snakes.

It was Penny—high up on her father's shoulders in the front of the line, taking it all in with that new vision of hers—it was Penny who first looked down and spied the hoof print. It was big, three or four inches across, and shadows pooled where the slanting afternoon sun found it. The impression lay in the shade of the grass and anyone else might have missed it. She tugged at the brim of her father's ball cap with one hand and pointed down with the other. "What made *that?*"

Weller stopped short, taking a hand away from balancing Penny and raising it palm out. "Whoa," he said, and Penny sang it out again, a couple of octaves higher. "Whoa!"

He bent over and she clambered down.

"Careful," he said. "You don't want to disturb anything."

"What is it?"

"I don't know."

"A bear?" She'd learned about bears from some of the books she'd had back home, storybooks her mother and father had saved and salvaged, picture books they'd made a custom of reading to her at bedtime. A family of three bears who lived in a cabin in the woods. A different bear who lived in a big city with trains that ran on tracks under the ground. Various others, in books complete and otherwise.

"No, sweetie. It's not a bear. Bears have paws, and this right here is a hoof."

She didn't know whether to be relieved or newly terrified, and neither did anyone else.

Whatever had made the print had been traveling northeast, its path crossing their slow southwesterly bend at a right angle. Weller bent himself double looking for another print, and although he didn't see one right away he saw something else instead—a dirt trail, halfway overgrown and not much used but a trail all the same. He followed it and found another print a few feet farther along. Not as close as he'd expected or hoped, but what did he know? If he had to guess, he'd guess that whatever animal had made it was moving fast. Behind him people were talking, asking questions, worrying out loud. He turned toward them and put a finger to his lips and waved the other hand to say *fan out*. To advise those following him not to cross the trail in one line but in many, so as to make their traces less visible.

Once upon a time he'd have followed the tracks—once upon a time when he had only himself to depend on and only himself to look after. When he was headed south from his imprisonment in Greensboro and he'd grown sick of being sneaked up on and had decided to take things into his own hands. But things were different now. All these people. They made a big target and out here in the wild they were as vulnerable as schoolchildren. Some of them actually were schoolchildren, his own included, but every one of them might as well have been. They were that innocent and that fragile. Somebody had to look after them. Somebody had to take responsibility.

Maybe Liz was right. She probably was. It wouldn't be the first time.

Everything was his fault.

So he picked up Penny and turned around in the grass and walked backward to make his shoes point in the direction from which he'd come, watching the rest of them do the same, fanning out behind him and crossing the trail with as little sign as possible.

*

"The main thing," he was saying as they rested through the long dead heat of the hour after noon, "is that we're not alone out here. And whatever it might be, it's pretty big. Wild horses, maybe. I doubt it'd be cattle. Seems to me the prints are too far apart for that. Regardless, we can't hunt it since we can't hunt anything, and trapping's out of the question. So all we can do is we keep our distance. Keep a low profile. Because whatever it is—and whatever people are involved with it, if there are any— we don't want trouble."

Everyone agreed.

"On the other hand," he went on, "the good news is that there's something out here besides us to catch Black Rose's attention. That's in our favor."

"We're not such an anomaly after all," said Dr. Patel. "There's some comfort in that. Good for us."

"Good for us."

"And there are always the runners, of course."

Weller wondered why she couldn't just let it go. Why she always had to bring everything back to the world as she'd come to understand it, whether or not the things she knew had any bearing on their present condition. It was a habit, he guessed, and a way of asserting herself. But it certainly didn't help. "Runners will stay out of sight," he said, trying to keep the focus on what was important. "These things are too big to do that."

"I was just saying we've never been alone anyhow."

"Right." He quit talking and sat down in the shade alongside Liz and Penny, deciding it was time he got the same rest everybody else was getting.

There *were* runners, of course. She was right about that. They hadn't seen any in all the time they'd been traveling, but that didn't mean there weren't plenty of them around. It was possible that they were keeping even more distance between themselves and the travelers than they would have kept under ordinary circumstances, since word had surely gotten out that Black Rose had attacked the research station and driven Patel's people into the wilderness. They'd draw trouble. They'd be poison. You didn't want to get mixed up with somebody that Black Rose had marked.

And there'd be more planes in the days to come, too. More planes high up and soundless with no signifier beyond their visible contrails. And lower down there'd be helicopters, a thousand times closer, close enough that you could practically feel the hammering pressure of their downdraft. But nothing airborne would ever give them any sign that they'd been spotted. So they kept on.

*

No matter how much time it cost them, they avoided roads. Increasingly it didn't matter anyhow, for as they moved west and then southwest and then fully south, down through the Appalachians across what had once been Pennsylvania, the roads merged back into the wilderness and the wilderness overtook the roads and everything became one again. It wasn't exactly the same as it had been before man had arrived here in the first place and made everything over into his own image and then abandoned it all, but it was close enough. Forest and meadow and rocky escarpment. You couldn't tell the road from the ruin.

They passed cities without names. Cities fallen and forested and filled in. A map might have helped and it might not, but all they had was Weller's old Black Rose compass anyhow. Rivers ran through the valleys and vanished into the fastnesses of the ruined cities as if into remote rain forests, passing over collapsed dams and beneath bridges as if into underground tunnels. Weller gave Penny a history lesson. People used to travel a route like this, he said, a couple of hundred years ago he was talking about, but in the opposite direction. Northbound. People just as secretive as they were. Which was difficult, given how many people were in these regions back in those days. The eighteen-hundreds if you could imagine that. People everywhere. Not just in the cities but in little towns and villages. Not even villages, sometimes, but individual cabins set on roads up into the mountains. Dirt roads, with a farm or a cabin or whatever at the end where somebody lived. The people going in secret, though, the people he was talking about, called the path they traveled the Underground Railroad.

Penny gasped, and her eyes went wider than usual. She'd seen railroad tracks on her way to New York with her father—or she'd kind of seen them, given that her vision had faded out almost entirely back then—and she'd seen them again on their panicky way back north in the big car that her father had gotten from Spartanburg for Mr. Carmichael, but even though she'd seen railroad tracks and a scattering of ruined cars she'd never seen an entire actual train. A whole train in motion. Never mind an *under-ground* train. An *underground railroad,* then, was pretty well past her ability to imagine. She said so.

Her father laughed. "It wasn't really underground," he said. "And it wasn't really a railroad."

She shook her head as if to clear the nonsense out of it. Silly grown-ups.

"Underground," he said, "meant secret."

"Like us."

"Like us. Exactly."

"As for the railroad part, I guess it was because they were transporting people."

"That's like us, too."

"A whole lot like us."

"Where were they going?"

"Up here into Pennsylvania. New York State. Even Canada." He told her how there'd been people down south who had kept other people like animals. Chained up and caged up and made to work in the fields whether they wanted to or not. Without pay. He said how these people, the ones kept like animals, were called slaves.

Penny stiffened, tightening her grip on him.

He took it to mean that she was worried about where they were headed, about getting caught up in some kind of trouble like that, and he told her those days were over. The slaveowners were all dead and gone. The country had fought a war over it, and the good guys had won.

Five:

Runners

Two men came down the mountain, moving fast over exposed rock. They had surely made an effort to conceal themselves higher up, and they would surely make such an effort again when they got back into the trees, but right now they were out in the open. Probably thinking what difference did it make. Nobody would be out here to see them anyhow, and the exposed face let them gain a little speed. The sinking western sun lit them against the rock and their shadows pursued them down the hill. Loose scree scattered with a distant shimmering sound from beneath their feet and one of them talked as they came, complaining in a voice that Weller and the rest could make out from the camp they were making in a wooded hollow below.

One of the women looked up from leafy shade and pointed toward them, saying "Runners." What else could they be? They had all the marks. The ragged clothing, the bony frames wasted away to almost nothing at all, the heavy backpacks loaded up with goods for the black market.

Their path down the mountainside would bring them close, perhaps even funneling them right into the camp. Just before they reentered the trees, Patel found a pair of binoculars and got in closer on their faces. Not close enough. She shook her head and clucked. She said they might be familiar and then again they might not.

There was always turnover among runners. You could make real money at it if you were fast enough and cunning enough and sufficiently lacking in regard for anyone but yourself, but it wasn't a life's work by any means. The smart ones got out when they could, and the ones who weren't that smart got killed or worse. So there was always attrition, and there were always plenty of new volunteers to take the places of those who'd gone before.

*

The travelers were hungry. The parents in particular, since they tended to share their own rations with their children. Dr. Patel was clear about why they should resist the urge, why it was crucial that every individual keep his strength up, but love will overcome reason every single time.

"If she had any children of her own," Liz said to Weller, "she'd know that you can't ask people not to feed their kids first."

"But she does," he said. "She sent them to India to be with their father, back before the Great Dying, and they never came home. She never had the money to follow them, either. Not once PharmAgra used her up and threw her away."

Liz's eyes grew as wide as Penny's. Like mother, like daughter. *"No,"* she said, aghast. "She didn't work for PharmAgra."

"She did. She worked on tobacco. That's how she got a leg up on dis-engineering the stuff in the first place."

Liz said that must mean Patel had a brand. Those devices of metal and plastic and silicon, embedded in your throat and used to connect you to everything. To your employer and to your medical records and to your finances, assuming you had any of the above. Back in the hospital in New York they'd tried installing one in Penny, but Liz hadn't let them. She'd read the consent forms and crossed out that line. The doctor had made her feel small for it. Made her feel as if she weren't doing her part. He'd reminded her that nobody had done the kind of work they were doing on Penny since just before the Great Dying, when weird illnesses and freak disabilities and hideous birth defects were cropping up all over the place like weeds and the doctors had their hands full. Branding her would be doing the world a favor, he said. It would be like tagging a migratory bird, back when there were plenty of birds around and scientists wondered how they lived. Or back when the birds began to disappear and scientists wondered where they were going. Liz had said she didn't care. She didn't want her daughter branded. Her daughter wasn't some migratory bird. Penny Weller wasn't some curiosity to be analyzed and understood.

Since the doctor had been talking about tracking wildlife, Liz had gotten the idea that there was some long-range locating function built into people's brands. She raised that idea to her husband now, saying, "If Patel's branded, then they can track her. They can find us."

"But she's not," he said. "She got laid off just before all that."

"You're sure."

"I'm sure."

Liz didn't look happy. She looked as if she were the only person among them who'd discovered the thing that would bring them all low. A prophet without honor in her own land.

"Plus," he said, "there's no tracking built into those things. What would be the point? People just use them to get into their jobs or buy stuff. Do their banking. If you were designing a thing like that, why would you bother with functionality you're not going to use?" Talking now like the mechanic he was.

She didn't look convinced.

"I had one myself for a while. Honest. Not in my neck, but in my pocket. I took it from a guy. Nobody tracked me with it."

"Maybe nobody wanted to."

"They wanted to all right. But they didn't. I figure they couldn't."

She turned away and started gathering up pine boughs, making a place to sleep beneath the trees.

He gave her a hand. "You feel better now?"

"I'll feel better," she said, "when we're all finally settled down."

*

They came through the underbrush and into the camp without hesitation. Two men beneath heavy packs, weary and dirty and worn down by their transit of the mountains. Worn down by everything, including the choices they'd made in this life and the world that had made such choices necessary. There was no fat on them, no excess of any sort, and they looked to have been thrown together from rawhide and old rope. They stank, but everybody stank.

Weller moved forward to meet them. There is a line between meeting and welcoming, and he didn't cross it. Weller had never been a big man but he'd always had a certain gravity about him, a weight that was undiminished by the trials he'd been through. If anything, it had been reinforced. He'd been sharpened like a knife. And these tough traveling men who would have thought nothing of him or less than nothing before were arrested by his presence now.

Liz watched him confront them. Confront them without confronting them exactly.

"How're you fellows doing?" he said. Asking it not as if he cared, but as if he had a right to know where they'd been and where they were going. What they meant by passing through here.

The taller of them took a long drink from a battered old military canteen that looked as if it had fallen to earth before the dawn of man.

The shorter one said they were doing fine. Just fine, thank you. Not daring to ask even the most inoffensive question in return.

Weller didn't say anything, didn't ask anything, just stood watching with one eyebrow raised.

The shorter one licked his lips watching the taller one drink. He pulled at the straps of his pack and shrugged a little, shifting the weight on his back. And after a minute he went on. "We come over from Jersey."

Weller didn't look interested, which meant he hadn't heard enough to care yet.

"There's farms down there everybody pretty much forgot." He winked.

Weller turned toward Patel. "Hey, Doc," he called "you know these two?"

She squinted over and shook her head.

The taller one was handing the canteen to the shorter one. Maybe now that he'd wet his whistle he'd talk. Weller left it pretty open. "You fellows know a lot about farming?"

"We might know about a few people who might do it." The taller one looked as if he wished he'd plugged his partner's mouth with the lip of the canteen. Weller was going to have to work to get any more information out of him.

"You got names?"

"No sir. They don't tell us their names." Looking at Weller as if he were an idiot for asking. As if he could leverage this to his advantage.

"I don't mean your customers. I mean you. You got names?"

The taller one hesitated.

"I'm Bud," said the shorter one. "This here's McCall."

McCall didn't say anything.

Weller didn't say anything.

"Anyhow," Bud said, "we're Scranton bound."

"Good for you," said Weller. "You must be close."

"I'd think a fellow like you would know that," McCall put in.

"I'd know it if I had any interest in Scranton." It was both a means of defense and a statement of truth. "But I don't."

"Good," said McCall. "Let's keep it that way." Glaring more at Bud than at Weller.

*

The runners settled in. They kept to themselves, dropping their packs and spreading their bedrolls at the far end of the camp where they could take off early in the morning without bothering anyone. Patel wandered over and made conversation. Dropping a few names and seeing if they made any impression. A couple of them did, at least on Bud, although McCall nodded ever so reluctantly too. Bud said he'd been partnered up with one of the men she mentioned a couple of years back. The fellow was dead now, he said. Quit the business and died from boredom, ha ha ha. It made sense to Patel, who hadn't seen the fellow in question for a long time. He'd been old already. He'd probably just run out of steam.

Bud said he'd been in business with McCall practically ever since that other fellow quit. They had a regular route, from South Jersey up here into PeeYay and then back on down into West Virginia. Over to Jersey again. A few little stops along the way. Sure, he said, it was long—but it was worth it. You couldn't mind going the distance and still run for a living. You couldn't have people at home you missed. You couldn't even have a home, not really. Not beyond your own bedroll.

He was a do-it-yourself philosopher, she decided. Time on the trail was time to think. Time in camp was time to talk.

She decided the two of them were all right, and she told Weller so. She said there was nothing to worry about.

*

Weller was up most of the night anyway. Sleeping with one eye open, which wasn't sleeping at all. He lay back on his elbows and watched the stars move overhead behind silhouetted leaves and black branches as still as carvings. Before long he grew resentful of how the runners were getting the very sleep that they were keeping him from. It wasn't fair. So he got quietly to his feet, listened for a second to make sure that he hadn't roused Penny or Liz, and made his way to their end of the camp.

He picked the tall one, McCall. He'd just about buried himself in his bed of leaves and pine needles, burrowed down halfway by either reflex or intent, concealed in the mold and rot like a withered corpse. Weller didn't want to take any chances. The man might be ready for anything. He might be armed—whether with a gun or a knife didn't matter much in the dark. And even if he didn't have a weapon handy, a person who slept that soundly under these circumstances must be pretty certain about his ability to handle himself. So he picked up a handful of loose dirt and tossed it. McCall rolled over and swatted at the air around his face with one hand. Weller tossed another handful and McCall was up, a long knife in his hand and nothing whatsoever in his eye. Not that you could see. Nothing but deadness and dark.

"Take it easy," said Weller. "I just thought we could have a little talk."

Nothing from McCall.

"Pass the time."

"Right," said McCall. Settling back. He cleared his throat, brushed some of the leaves and needles from his pantlegs. "Since my partner told you everything there is to know about us," he said, "I guess you can go first. Where're you folks bound, anyway?"

Weller said they were heading south.

"Steer clear of Greensboro," said McCall.

Which sat all right with Weller, because he knew from experience that it was good advice. He nodded in the dark as if he were making a mental note.

"As a rule," McCall said, "we won't go farther south than Harrisonburg. All kinds of weird stuff beyond that."

"Weird stuff," said Weller.

McCall clammed up. Maybe he'd been saying too much.

"I guess you don't go to North Carolina, then. You don't go to Spartanburg."

McCall blew air in something like a laugh. "Spartanburg? Nobody goes there."

"Nobody?"

"It's a goddamned armed camp. Black Rose won't even get close."

"They must get food from someplace," said Weller. "Somebody must go there."

"Nobody I ever heard of. I'd guess they're pretty well self-contained."

Honest answers, as far as they went. No mythology and no nonsense. Weller decided that there was no point in stretching this out. He didn't want to mislead McCall about his own experience or intentions. What he wanted was to trust McCall and for McCall to trust him in return. It made life easier. It confirmed his opinion that there were some good people in the world. "I'll tell you the truth," he said, "Spartanburg's right where we're headed." Trading one thing for another, the way you do in conversation.

Even in the dark, the look in McCall's eye said Weller was crazy. "I can't imagine why," he said. "There's plenty of other places."

"Not like Spartanburg."

"Screw Spartanburg. You'll never get in. They'll shoot you a hundred yards out, or else they'll just let you beat your head against the wall until you get tired and go on home."

"How would you know?"

"Everybody knows."

"Maybe what everybody knows is wrong."

McCall just shook his head. Taking pity on Weller and the rest of them, out here risking their lives on a fool's errand.

Weller leaned toward him and set his voice even lower he'd set it already. All that remained was a whisper and a hiss. "I've been there," he said. "I've been inside."

"I took you for an honest man. A little crazy, but honest. Now I don't know what to think."

"Think whatever you like," said Weller.

"I will."

"It won't change the facts."

McCall shrugged. "Facts. I've been out here long enough to know the facts. But hey, you're free to go wherever you want. It's no skin off my nose."

By now Bud was waking up, pushing away leaves and stretching out to his full length which wasn't much. Moving with the resignation of a man to whom it didn't matter what time it was, once you were awake you might as well get moving. Time was money, or AmeriBank scrip, or whatever else you could get your hands on.

McCall called over to him. "Turns out this fellow knows all there is to know about Spartanburg."

"How'd that come up?"

"We were just talking. He says he's been there. Inside."

Bud whistled low. "Now I heard everything."

"That's what I said."

Bud came over, brushing pine needles off the seat of his pants. "You're welcome to it," he said. "Spartanburg's a little beyond our territory, if you know what I mean."

"Keep an open mind," said Weller.

Six:

Murdering History

It was still mostly dark when the runners packed up and left, down into a rolling landscape that would be a thousand times easier to traverse than the mountain passages they'd left behind. Weller watched them go. He leaned against a tree and kept an eye on the spot where they'd vanished into the leaves and down a trail that wasn't a trail at all by any normal standard, standing guard in case they doubled back for some reason. But they didn't. He was sleeping there when the sun came up and his own crowd began moving around. Penny found him on the dirt, slid down among sprawling roots, snoring.

The world grew warmer as they moved south and west. Somewhere along the way they crossed the Mason Dixon, although at a great remove from the vast transportation hubs of Philadelphia and Wilmington where the trucks rolled day and night and the mighty PharmAgra processing plants stood fuming, leaching out the poisons engineered into food grown throughout the Northeastern Empowerment Zone. That was PharmAgra's singular achievement: the poisoning of food not only against the usual threats of insects and rot, but against the very people who planted and cultivated it. A true marvel of engineering and science. Plants that couldn't sustain themselves without technical assistance, and people who couldn't sustain themselves either. From this—from scarcity and limitation and threat—they drew their enormous power.

There was a certain happy coincidence behind it all. The technicians at PharmAgra—and at NutraMax prior to that, where Dr. Patel had worked before the economy collapsed and the world got big again and she found herself alone and out of work in America with her husband and children unreachable in Bangalore—the technicians who'd modified the genetic code of every crop known to man had not begun with the idea of making them poisonous to people. It just turned out that way. It turned out that the very same mutations that killed bugs also killed human beings. An unintended consequence. But don't blame the scientists. By and large they did their work and turned in their disappointing results and waited for clearance to pursue research along other paths. Clearance that never came, once the marketing gurus and the financial planners and the investment bankers got hold of the facts. The scientists could have found another way. There's little doubt of that. But the marketers and the planners and the bankers liked the idea of turning poisoned lemons into poisoned lemonade.

So it became a gold rush. A one-company gold rush. PharmAgra began quietly buying everybody in sight. Not just NutraMax, but everybody. They bought competing pharmaceutical and agricultural companies that were still thinking small—thinking, that is, that the methodical murder of innocent people was probably not a sustainable business plan. They bought little mom and pop seed companies that lacked for distribution but still kept big stocks of antique and heirloom seeds around, stocks that were easy enough to destroy. They bought seed banks and gene banks, and one by one they eliminated them too. They didn't even keep records of everything they'd ruined. They didn't trust anybody with that kind of information. Not even themselves. They were forging a brave new world, and there would be no going back to the old one. They were murdering history.

Nature played a part, too—resourceful nature, which as it happens can be driven out more completely with a mass spectrophotometer than with a pitchfork. Insect populations that couldn't adapt to the newly engineered crops found organic ones that even PharmAgra couldn't track down, hidden stashes here and there as rare as gemstones, and when they were finished with them the crops were gone for good. The illnesses and mutations that engineered food brought on began to thrive on their own, passing from gene to gene and hijacking otherwise innocent viruses and bacteria, bending them to their own distributive needs. In the end, the Great Dying wasn't one thing, it was all of these things. Engineered crops and swarming insects and evolving disease—in particular one deadly virus that raged through human populations like wildfire. Even PharmAgra had been unable to cure it.

If all roads once led to Rome, they led now to the Mason Dixon line where National Motors trucks roared day and night, racing down roadways emblazoned mile after mile with the company's red-star logo—just as PharmAgra owned the food and drug business, National Motors owned transit—delivering poisoned food to PharmAgra factories and bringing it back decontaminated, for sale to the people who'd planted it and cultivated it and harvested it to begin with. It was a sweet deal for those who'd gotten in early. For those with the vision and the power and the connections to have seen it coming and capitalized on it.

Moving south the travelers entered into places where the signs of civilization grew more and more common. Prior civilization, anyhow. Ruined commercial strips and empty suburban neighborhoods and collapsed industrial sites. Crumbled roads littered with cars and trucks that had run out of gas years before, cars and trucks that had been occupied for a while by people and then by animals and then by nothing at all except the air and the sunlight and the rain. Pipelines and oil tanks overgrown with green.

The National Motors highways out this far weren't even fenced—there was no one around to trespass on them, after all—and the travelers generally saw that as a kind of miracle. Instead of searching out a passable bridge or a navigable culvert, instead of cutting through the chain link fencing and risking detection by whatever electronic systems were no doubt monitoring everything up and down the line, they just crept up to the shoulder and looked both ways and dashed across. Liberty. There was nothing like it in the world.

*

On the third night, the runners crossed their paths again. The two men came from behind, along the same upward-sloping hollow the travelers had chosen as evening was coming on so as to gain a little height and perspective. There had been a road here once, a road that wound among tall trees, although all that it led to now was a ghostly realm of overgrown fields and tumbledown shacks. An abandoned cemetery overrun with vines. The mysterious skeletons of rusted farm equipment hidden among tall weeds.

Word went quickly around the camp. Weller figured that no matter what the runners might say, it was no coincidence that they were here. What they might say would tell him a lot, though. A lot about their intentions, whether they meant it to or not. So he left Penny and Liz, and sought them out.

"We got thinking about Spartanburg," the short one said right off. Bud.

"Thinking what?" Weller asked.

"Thinking maybe we ought to expand our territory some."

"Thinking you had some contacts down there," McCall put in, "and maybe we could take advantage of them."

Bud apologized for his partner. "Take advantage might be the wrong way to put it," he said.

"I understand," said Weller.

So they had a meeting. Everyone except the two runners, who went back on down the road into the gathering darkness so as not to overhear what might be said about them. The travelers whispered nonetheless, mostly about having two more mouths to feed with supplies running short already. Weller pointed out that they were looking at it wrong—that experienced runners could teach them all a thing or two about living off the land. Patel suggested how ironic it was that the tables had been turned, and that now they'd be leading a couple of individuals who by rights ought to know their own way around. Janey said she didn't care either way. The closer she got to home, the less certain she was that she wanted to go there anyhow—either with these two or without them. In her heart she wished she could see the great big world that they already knew, instead of having it the other way around.

Most of the rest of them, Liz included, just wanted to get it over with.

Seven:

Good For The Soul

Hutchinson would have to lie to cover up what happened in Connecticut. The destruction of that whole town and every last man, woman, and child in it. He'd need to make up a great many lies, because it was a bigger problem than any one lie would cover. He'd have help, though. Every man in every platoon would help, because nobody wanted to tell the truth. Nobody wanted to let on how it had turned from nothing into something so quickly.

He kept thinking back to that day, though. To the end of it, when the rain had begun and the whole town was a sucking wet bog of ashes and dirt and bodies far past identifying. A smudge on the map where there wasn't even a map.

It broke his heart to remember it, and it broke his heart to tell lies about it. But covering up misery was part of the job.

*

The hearings went upstairs one level at a time, headed all the way to General Bainbridge. Hutchinson told the same story every time, and the men who listened to him from behind their high desks all nodded the same way in response. As if it was just a memory test they were giving him and he was passing it. Qualifying for something. Their ranks went up with every telling, and as the repetitions went on there were more civilians listening.

Representatives of the stockholders. Members of the Board of Directors. Men and women both, people who didn't look as if they belonged here but belonged here because of the money they'd invested in Black Rose.

They were Ownership, and they were here to look after their investment, and that was the extent of their interest. The more of them there were behind the high desks the less Hutchinson liked it, because civilians always had trouble comprehending military problems. They would only be looking out for the bottom line. You couldn't run an army on the bottom line. You couldn't even make up a web of lies that made it seem that way, and he tried.

*

When the last hearing came, Hutchinson and Bainbridge were the only two in uniform. That didn't mean Hutchinson didn't say *yes, sir* and *no, sir* to everybody, but it felt strange when he did it. He said *yes, ma'am* and *no, ma'am* too, which felt even stranger although he didn't let it show. The presence of all these civilians didn't seem to trouble Bainbridge in the least. He acted right at home. He acted as if they were all one big happy family and he was the *paterfamilias*. Bainbridge and his five stars and his gold braid and his bristly little mustache with that famous big white smile gleaming underneath it. The stockholders were all deferential to him.

Hutchinson wondered if he had them tamed somehow, since they didn't look like a group of people who as a rule saw things the same way. They looked like people prone to conflict and disagreement. So he wondered what it was. Possibly they just respected an old man in a uniform with all those medals. Possibly they looked up to a person who'd been President Cheney's right hand all those years, chairman of the Joint Chiefs and so forth. Most likely they were just dependent like everybody else and they'd given him the reins so what the hell. He knew from experience that if you made decisions for people they usually let you get away with it. He quit wondering and somebody called the hearing to order and he started telling the stories he'd made up, just the way he'd told them before.

Bainbridge, hearing his testimony in person for the first time, didn't take it the same way everyone before him had. *"You don't have to bullshit me,"* was how he took it. Not even halfway through Hutchinson's testimony, and smiling that big smile of his. He was all teeth like Teddy Roosevelt in the history books. The one with the Rough Riders. Just a happy warrior, charging up some hill to deal out death like cards. "These nice folks only want to hear the truth, sonny. Isn't that right?" Looking around at the rest of them as if they all were in on it but weren't saying. As if everybody had been in on it all along, everybody Hutchinson had talked to in one hearing after another, and nobody had said.

It made the lie catch in Hutchinson's throat.

"Who're you looking out for?" Bainbridge asked. "You're covering for somebody. I want it to stop right here."

The men and women behind the high desks all came to attention, as if they were about to witness the revelation of something that nobody in the whole world had seen before. Some great truth. The kind of thing that a properly maintained military structure could force out of even a hard man like Hutchinson.

He cleared his throat. "General, sir—"

"I'm all ears." Smiling that smile.

"What happened out there, sir, it was—"

"No bullshit, now. You got that?"

"Yes, sir."

"Good. Go ahead, son."

"What happened, sir, was—"

"Because *somebody's* got to take the credit for this, and by God if you won't I will."

"Sir?"

Bainbridge rolled on like that Roosevelt, up the hill grinning. "Of course I'll get the credit either way, since good will always flows toward the top. But I wouldn't mind sharing a little bit with the fellow responsible."

"Credit, sir?"

"Plenty to go around." Bainbridge gave him a little wink that tugged at the old leather mask of his face. Then he looked from one of his fellows behind the high desks to another. "Ain't that right, folks?"

They all smiled. Man and woman, civilian and uniformed. They smiled like people who'd been sworn a long time ago to keep a secret that had had them just about bursting, and now it was coming out.

"Nobody blames you, son. It's not that way. You fellows did what needed doing."

Nodding all around.

Hutchinson sitting with his hands folded, pressing his forearms down onto the table top as a means of anchoring himself. Anchoring himself to the world where everything was shifting.

"If things got a little bit out of hand, so be it."

Pursed lips all around. Looks of sympathy not for the dead, but for the guilty living. *All is forgiven,* they said.

Bainbridge leaned forward a few degrees and fixed Hutchinson with a look. "I do have one question for you," he said.

"Sir?"

"How on earth are we ever supposed to surpass this months' billing?" With that big smile breaking out again.

Laughter erupted behind the high desks. The kind of irrepressible but transient delight that can come only from a sudden infusion of money or some other drug.

Over it, Bainbridge kept on. "You do understand what they call a *cost-plus contract,* don't you, son? Where the more you spend the more you make?"

"I believe I do, sir."

"Then you'll understand that our friends at AmeriBank will be digging a little deeper than usual this quarter. Just the markup on the ammo alone. And half of that stuff, if you'll forgive my mentioning it, was so damn old it's a miracle it worked at all."

One of the civilians, a dignified lawyer type with a bald head and a serious manner, raised his hand for clearance from Bainbridge and put in, "We'll actually be reopening the armory in Fairfax in order to restock. Those are jobs we thought we'd lost forever." He gave Hutchinson a friendly little salute. "Thanks to you and your men, sir, we're back in business."

Bainbridge beamed.

Hutchinson looked up, searching from face to face for even one hint of disapproval. He found nothing of the kind. "Begging the general's pardon," he said after a minute. "People made mistakes out there. I admit that one of my intentions in coming here was to conceal that."

"You're among friends," said Bainbridge.

"But you said no bullshit, sir."

"And I meant it."

"All right, then," said Hutchinson. "Here it is. The operation in Connecticut went sideways rapidly, once a number of the men grew impatient with the locals. They drew their weapons when they shouldn't have, and they fired when they shouldn't have, and as terrible as it is that kind of thing often proves contagious. The locals, on the other hand, were completely unarmed and entirely innocent."

"According to whom?"

"According to me, sir. According to everyone who was there."

"Not according to the record," said Bainbridge. As if the record were some independent power that overruled everything else—common sense and truth included.

Hutchinson was not deterred. "They were my men," he went on, "and I failed them, and in their defense I came here to lie to you. To say there was a good reason for what happened, when there wasn't. There couldn't be."

"That's noble of you, my boy. God bless you for coming clean."

More nodding from behind the high desks.

Bainbridge pushed his chair back a couple of inches, signaling that this session was about to wind down. "As good as confession is for the soul," he said, "I'd advise you—from a practical standpoint—that there's a limit to everything. Wallowing in it won't bring those people back. And since we're indemnified against loss of life, any problem that PharmAgra might have with the whole business will go straight to the insurers." He clapped his hand on the desktop. "That's it, son. You're dismissed. The boys in payroll will zap you your bonus right away." He stood, and he thanked Hutchinson for his continuing service, and that was that.

*

Even though he knew it was impossible, Hutchinson swore he could feel the bonus payment the very instant it arrived. It felt as if the little spot near his Adam's apple were vibrating all of a sudden. He knew that a brand didn't have any moving parts. There wasn't a buzzer inside it. There wasn't anything that could have gotten jogged loose. It was just a little antenna and a wireless receiver and a microchip or two. But it felt that way now. It felt as if it wanted attention.

He'd never given his brand much thought before. He'd received it as an adult, when he'd joined Black Rose. Hutchinson hadn't been an Ownership or Management baby, that was for sure. He'd grown up rough like anybody else. Out there on the southernmost edge of the Northeastern Empowerment Zone, down by the Mason Dixon line where PharmAgra had their factories. People called them *plants* without any irony whatsoever. This agricultural company treating its crops in a factory to make them edible by the very people who'd raised them.

Hutchinson's father had worked on the highway. Maintenance with a shovel and a pick. It was hard labor on hot tar under a blistering sun, the kind of thing that road gangs made up of criminals used to do in the same place a hundred years before him. Criminals bound together by ankle chains or by the presence of a man with a long rifle. Men atoning for something they hadn't planned on getting caught at, hard men and angry men and desperate men reduced to putting in time before their lives could get started once more. Working and waiting.

Hutchinson's father hadn't gotten caught doing anything but living an ordinary life. He'd been a storekeeper before the Great Dying. He'd had a hobby shop in a little strip mall outside Baltimore until nobody needed hobbies anymore. A person with a hobby had time on his hands, and nobody had time anymore. He'd look back on those old days as he shoveled a half-ton of pea gravel into the back of a National Motors truck and it would seem to him as if he were looking back at a world that had never existed at all. As if he were looking back at a dream he'd had. Trying to reconstruct it but the pieces wouldn't hold together. Still he remembered details. How they'd burned everything they could burn right up until the end. How he'd thought about raising the price of turpentine and white gas and model airplane fuel until he realized that there wasn't any point saving up money when there wouldn't be anything left to buy in the world that was coming, and how that very day he'd just opened the doors and let it all go. Shed himself of it. Freed himself. And in his freedom he'd gone to work on the National Motors road gang.

Hutchinson remembered the transformation. He remembered the years when his father had driven off every day to the hobby shop, and then he remembered a dark period when he quit using the car and stayed home half the time and the house was filled with argument, and finally he remembered watching the old man go off to work on foot, his back bent and his spirit broken. That red National Motors star on his armband.

The job wasn't a Management job but he'd treated it as if it was, wearing that armband with something almost like pride. So he didn't have a brand and Hutchinson's mother didn't have one either. They went to their graves unmarked and unimproved and undefiled. If you were to locate them now and dig them up, they could be anybody. You could sift through their remains and come upon no sign.

Hutchinson had a brand. A glistening square with metal prongs on either side, mounted in rubber, the signifier of Black Rose. He'd never seen it, of course, but he'd seen others. In Basic Training, every new recruit had to learn the quickest and most foolproof way to extract a brand from a fellow soldier's neck, just in case worse came to worst. You didn't leave anybody's brand on the field of battle. You could leave his body but not his brand. An enemy could do only so much with a body. A brand, though, that was different. A brand was a passcode and medical history and a bank account all rolled into one, and you could cause some real trouble with one that didn't belong to you. Take that guy Weller they'd been looking for. There were stories. Stories that Hutchinson couldn't decide were just the usual bullshit you hear, or something else. The beginnings of some kind of myth.

*

He actually remembered Weller. Not personally or anything. Just from seeing him around the Pentagon and knowing who he was. Their paths had crossed a couple of times in the mess hall and in the gym, back when Weller was getting his Black Rose training. Getting it straight from old man Bainbridge himself, under contract. It seemed like a million years ago but it must have been what, no more than a few months. Things changed fast.

You didn't think anything could change much at all anymore, with the whole world so locked down. Ownership on top with the resources, and Management underneath with the jobs, and then everybody else at the bottom with nothing. *Generics.* Which was what Hutchinson was, before he pulled himself up by his own bootstraps and joined Black Rose. Black Rose was the only way an outsider could get in. The only way a generic could earn himself a brand. Rise up above where his people had fallen.

He remembered Weller, though, at least a little. Everybody had called him the Sacrificial Lamb, but not to his face. Even Bainbridge. It was a big joke. How that greedy bastard who ran AmeriBank wanted some car that nobody else had, just to show how much better he was than anybody, and how Weller had volunteered to get it for him from those murderous lunatics down in Spartanburg. Apparently no one had told Mr. AmeriBank that it was impossible. That Spartanburg was an armed camp where Black Rose hadn't gone for years. That Spartanburg was a place where you let sleeping dogs lie.

The funny thing, though, was that the joke turned out to be on them. Because nobody had told the Sacrificial Lamb that the whole deal was impossible, either. Or maybe somebody had, and the Sacrificial Lamb saw it differently. Either way he proved them wrong. He had an agenda of his own, that was for sure. Nobody did something like that for money. Nobody in his right mind, and by all accounts he was every bit in his right mind. You couldn't take that away from him. He was just a little deluded and naïve. Another disposable nobody in the service of Ownership. You met them every day. They were you, if you weren't careful.

Word was that it had something to do with his daughter. That banker had made a promise that he'd do something for Weller's daughter, provided he got him the car. Nobody gave a shit about that. Black Rose didn't care about the daughter or about the father either. He was a paycheck and a big one. Bainbridge kept him here at Black Rose HQ in Washington, the old public White Washington of granite and marble, training him up for the duty as best he could. Almost caring but not quite. The longer he stayed, the more income he generated—and Bainbridge certainly cared about that.

When Weller was as ready as he was ever going to get they sent him off on a rusty old sorry-ass Harley Davidson motorcycle left over from World War II, straight into the belly of some beast they feared without limit. That rickety old motorcycle. He didn't know where they'd found it in the first place. But you didn't send good hardware off on a mission with the Sacrificial Lamb.

*

When the hearings were done Hutchinson had orders to return to his unit. The Humvee they'd assigned him was in a remote lot, out near the old Lincoln Memorial. He walked there across the bridge, and he climbed in and turned the key and sat behind the wheel feeling the engine roaring away alongside his right hip, waiting for the choke to cut itself off if it ever would. The whole truck threatening to vibrate itself to pieces. He put down the window to let some heat out and to let some different heat in, thinking that if Black Rose had had any sense they'd have taken that Weller on board while he was available. Put him to work in the motor pool, if he was as good as they said he was. He tapped the accelerator but the choke stayed on. The steering wheel shaking under his hands. The only advantage of sitting in this damned earth tremor on wheels was it took his mind off the brand in his neck. How could the brand seem to vibrate with that kind of competition?

He sat there thinking of it by trying not to think of it. Thinking of the physicality of the steel and rubber and silicon lodged in his throat. Thinking of the bonus that Bainbridge had promised and that the payroll folks had surely zapped into his account just the way he'd said they would. Black Rose scrip stored there now as zeroes and ones.

Wondering how much it was. How much extra they'd seen fit to pay him.

Wondering how many men and women and children he'd left dead on the dead ground in Connecticut.

If you knew the number of them and you knew how big his bonus was, you could calculate the value of a human life.

He pictured the brand in his neck and his blood pumping past it. He wondered how much blood every day. How much blood and how much time it would take for that much blood to wash away that much stain.

He'd started out a few days prior telling lies on behalf of his men, but in the end it turned out that all he'd been lying for was money. Treasure and blood mixed up together the way they always were.

He put the Humvee into gear and he went, only he didn't go back to his unit. He didn't know exactly where he'd go. Someplace where he could wash himself clean..

Eight:

Homecoming

When they came near the car factory from out of the deep woods, Janey didn't even recognize it. She'd never seen it from the outside, except for once in a rear view mirror. The passenger side rear view of the big sleek BMW X9 that she and Weller had been in the process of driving north. She'd been too busy then to pay the building much attention. Too busy looking for land mines and trip wires. But now that she was back and seeing it from an entirely new perspective the experience was a shock. It was like seeing your mother for the first time after you'd spent nine months inside her body—except in Janey's case it wasn't nine months. It was twenty-some years, and she'd never once had a clear picture of where she'd spent them. That converted car factory. Marlowe's Retreat. Spartanburg or what was left of it.

She'd seen out from its walls, though, out through a couple of barred windows in the barracks and out by means of some cameras on a crackling feed in the Comm Center. She'd seen the desolation. The scorched earth that encircled the place like a curse or the wrath of God, death radiating out a mile in every direction and the factory itself Ground Zero. She remembered looking out toward the treeline, gray trees in the black and white Comm Center monitors or green trees made gray by the rising dust clouds visible from the barred windows. She remembered seeing in between the factory and the treeline a maze of hurricane fence and razor wire, a treacherous forest of it designed to repel infiltration or attack. Built to deter the unwelcome or the unwholesome or the unliving in their efforts to intrude upon paradise.

Of course there were no such threats. She knew that now.

Everybody knew that now, apparently. Because there were people outside the car factory, laboring in the sunshine that poured down freely from the clear blue sky. There were two crews of them, one dismantling the last of the fences and wire, the other preparing the soil. The first crew working with their hands and the other using a couple of those little green John Deere tractors they seemed to think would last forever.

She stood in the shade of those encircling trees and watched them as they worked, waiting for everybody else to catch up. Waiting above all for Weller, who'd converted those selfsame tractors to run on ethanol when he was here a thousand years ago. Before they'd cut the door open with an acetylene torch and blown the cover off a secret that had been kept for more or less a generation and changed everything. *Let my people go.*

*

Bud caught up with Janey before Weller did. Weller was back with his wife and child, going slowly and carefully, but Bud moved right along. He always did. He had just one speed, which you might call urgent. It was the pace of a man carrying something he shouldn't be carrying, in between places he didn't have any business going. McCall had the same pace. Every runner did, more or less. When you stopped being able to maintain it, you stopped being a runner. You stopped of your own free will or someone stopped you.

Bud was probably ten years older than Janey but he looked twice that distance, worn down and wrung out the way runners get. He was shorter than McCall and his walk had a kind of busyness about it that McCall's didn't have. If you were to bet money on them you'd bet that McCall had more years left in him than Bud, if only because his strides were longer and moving across the landscape seemed to cost him less effort. But Bud didn't let it show. He wasn't even panting when he broke through the trees and joined Janey at the edge of the circle of bare earth. Astonished to see people where he'd been led to believe there'd be nothing but a walled fortress.

"What else ain't the way I expected it?" he asked nobody. "What other lies they been telling me, huh?"

"I never lied to you."

"I ain't saying *you* did."

Janey stood watching people work. They were still at some distance, so she couldn't say she recognized anyone. She would, though, when they got closer. Everybody in Spartanburg knew everybody else. There weren't that many of them. "Nobody lied to you," she said. "It wasn't like this. Just a few weeks ago it wasn't. I never thought it would change."

"The Eternal City," said Bud. It was something he'd heard. He thought it might have meant New York. He thought it might have meant heaven.

"I thought it was. But it changed. They opened the doors."

"A place ain't got an open door, it ain't nothing but a prison."

"You're right" Looking from the car factory to Bud, imagining everything he'd seen in the world that she hadn't been able to. "It didn't feel like a prison, but it was."

"I'll never know how you stood it." A man of the world, admiring this girl for something she actually didn't have anything to do with. For strength she'd never claimed.

One of the tractors stopped short, and she realized that she was still too far away to hear whether it kept running or not. Her old friends and neighbors were like people on the moon. That remote and that isolated from where she was and where she'd been. Where she had yet to go.

*

Weller couldn't believe his eyes either, but it was better than what he'd expected, which was that they'd find the factory locked down tight again—locked down tighter than ever, if that were possible. Oates having withdrawn further into his armored shell and taken everybody with him. He didn't know exactly how they would have found their way inside again if that had been the case. Sure, he'd promised Patel that everything would be all right, that there would be no problem whatsoever, but he knew he'd been taking on a lot by saying it. He'd gotten used to taking on a lot. He'd been through the wars, and the wars weren't over yet.

"I wonder who was the first person to step outside," he said to Janey. "The first one to get up the nerve." Standing there amazed on the treeline, shaking his head. "The doors weren't alarmed, were they? I don't remember."

"Alarmed? They weren't even *doors.*" She was right. The loading docks had been welded shut a long time ago, back when Marlowe and his followers had taken over the empty factory. The people they'd left behind in the crumbling outer world had decided to call it Marlowe's Retreat, first the action and then the mythical place itself. They made up stories about it—stories good and bad, stories comforting and terrifying—rather than let themselves forget that there was someplace other than where they were. Where there was someplace else, there was hope.

Nobody had actually seen Marlowe in ages. Nobody outside Spartanburg and nobody inside. In that way you might say that Janey and Weller could call themselves lucky, for they were the exceptions. They'd seen him in the flesh, prisoner of his own age and infirmity, prisoner of his second-in-command Oates, prisoner of the place he'd built for his own salvation. They'd broken into his quarters and found him, hooked up to oxygen and pinned to his bed by his own weakness while Oates went on manufacturing stories about his ongoing heroism and command.

"I wonder if he's even *alive,*" said Janey, and they both knew who she was talking about.

*

They all felt ill at ease as they left the shade of the treeline and put themselves willfully out in the open. They'd grown so accustomed to secrecy. Not just Bud and McCall, but everyone. They scanned the treeline as it opened around them. They studied the ground, which proved to be made up of dirt hummocks and knocked-down masonry and the foundations of old roadways. They sought hiding places where there were none and they calculated escape routes where escape was impossible. *Escape from what* was the question. From nothing in particular. From everything. Just as Marlowe had escaped from everything so long ago. Just as he had escaped to here.

Penny saw the memorial first, down a straight lane graded in the jumbled dirt. Straight and level to the treeline, westward. In the direction where the sun would set and the future would lie. What she saw was a place cut clear in the woods and planted over with grass that was just coming in. A little treed temple with a square stone standing upright in the middle.

She pointed and her father knew. "That'll be him," he said. "That'll be Marlowe under that rock."

Nine:

Marlowe's Retreat

Marlowe's reputation, they discovered as they skirted the factory and drew nearer to the crews who were working the raw earth, was undiminished by death. Death had in fact burnished his standing. An official portrait of him hung over the loading dock doors. It didn't hang, actually. It was painted on, looming upward at a grand scale that stretched three or four stories. Men with ladders were still working on it, mapping color onto a grid of squares.

The portrait showed Marlowe in his prime, with an immovable set to his jaw and an optimistic gleam in his eye. He looked fierce and farsighted. Someone not to be trifled with and someone to be depended upon. Weller sized him up and realized why lesser individuals called what he'd accomplished here his *retreat*. Because even if the portrait exaggerated his qualities by half, he was clearly someone to whom retreat was unthinkable.

His detractors, men like Bainbridge, had diminished him in their minds but not in reality. Not in the world, and the world was what mattered. They feared him and they knew it, and so they mocked him. Mocked him because they knew he would never return to defend himself. He would never return because he didn't need to.

Unless Weller was letting the power of that portrait get the better of him.

He'd seen the real live Marlowe himself, after all, gasping for air in that upstairs bedroom. Gasping for air and crying out Oates's name.

*

Janey went first. The rest of them hung back some distance, not lined up in any way, certainly not arrayed like any sort of threat, just standing quietly in the rubble and whispering low to one another across little open spaces. A couple of them swatted at their arms and legs without even recognizing that there were bugs here. Just killing for their own comfort, with no thought to it at all.

Weller was sure that people would recognize him well enough once Janey got things rolling. He hadn't been around for long but he figured he'd made an impression, especially among the folks who operated the tractors. As for McCall and Bud, they slipped behind other men and froze the same way they'd have frozen behind trees.

The workers craned their necks and squinted toward Janey as she came closer. Recognition bloomed on their faces one after another. *She's back. We'd never thought.* And after every recognition there came a question. *If she's back, where's she back from? What might she have seen?* A million ideas and a million questions dancing across their faces like lightning.

And then they erupted toward her. Some dropped their tools to the ground and some held on to them, lifting up rakes and hoes and spades and running. Bud flinched to see it unfold and McCall did too, cringing and drawing into themselves as if confronted by something enormous that was about to fall to pieces. Something that threatened not just Janey but all of them. Reflexes on that order had kept them alive more than once, and it took a willful effort to relax once conditions had shown their true nature. Smiles all around. Smiles and voices uplifted. Something in the base of their spines didn't know what to make of it.

*

They set out a feast, with tables running the full length of the residential district. Everyone pitched in, until you couldn't say whose idea it might have been or who was in charge. Everyone and no one. It was as if their favorite child had returned home after a long and uncertain absence. One of their own had gone away and now she was back. They were restored.

Oates arrived to preside over the evening. The dinner had materialized from nowhere and he did the same, and at his appearance the crowd parted. Weller almost didn't recognize him. He wasn't wearing his uniform. He looked like a man who'd never worn a uniform. Instead he had a pair of bib overalls, like the lowliest of field hands. They weren't new, but nothing was new. Someone else had worn them before, worn them hard, and they bore the signs of it. Underneath he had a white shirt with the sleeves rolled up above his elbows. As if he'd been working deep in something. Maybe he had.

But it wasn't just his appearance. It was the way people responded to him. When Weller was here the first time, people had taken orders from Oates because he was the highest-ranking individual around. He had exclusive access to Marlowe, and he spoke therefore with untranslated or at least unchallenged authority, and his word was law. But now it was different. Now his word was something more like gospel. He spoke softly and patiently, giving counsel instead of commanding, and people leaned in to hear. They tilted their heads so as not to miss a syllable, as if fearing that some nuance might escape them.

It was a brand new era in Spartanburg. But Weller could see that Oates was still in charge.

*

McCall and Bud hung back, whispering. The tables that lined the street were spread with foods that had long ago vanished into rumor. Heirloom tomatoes and corn on the cob. Green salads untainted and unprocessed. Roast chicken and mashed potatoes with fresh yellow butter pooling on the side.

They couldn't begin to imagine what such treasures might be worth on the open market. It was incalculable. They weren't thieves, though. Not as a rule, or at least not entirely. Runners didn't steal because they didn't need to steal and more than that they didn't steal because they couldn't afford to. What they needed on a regular basis was to keep the wheels of commerce greased, and that meant treating their customers more or less fairly. If you stole from somebody, you stole once—and there weren't that many opportunities left in the world.

Still, this was tempting.

It was a long trip down here, though. Like the old spice routes across Asia. People used words like *spice routes across Asia* without knowing exactly what they once meant, but they still meant something. It was a long haul between Spartanburg and anywhere, and you'd have to make a major profit on a trip like that for it to be worthwhile. Who had the resources? Not the generics that runners worked for. Not Management either. And Ownership already had everything they needed. They had more than they needed. They had damned pineapples from Hawaii, if what you heard was true. Flown in. You couldn't get pineapples in Spartanburg. Tell Ownership about some heirloom tomatoes—if you could get within a mile of their barricaded cities—and they'd laugh in your face. *Enjoy your tomatoes, little man. We've got all the pineapples we can eat.*

Ten:

The Open City

Oates moved through the crowd toward Janey, and once he'd collected her he began working his way toward Weller. He kept his head down, whispering something in her ear, and although she looked uncomfortable in what was amounting to an embrace there was nothing she could do about it. He was an old man but he was powerful. Janey understood that whatever transformation he had undergone he had undergone without her around, and she was going to have to catch up fast. Catch up or be left behind scratching her head, wondering what everybody else saw.

"Henry," he called when they got near Weller. He'd never called him *Henry*. As far as Weller could recall, he might never have called him anything. Weller had been unworthy of a name, just an intruder and an irritant to be eliminated as quickly as possible, and now all of a sudden he was *Henry*, with a big welcoming smile. Henry, his oldest pal. "You did us all a great kindness, Henry," he went on. "I don't know how I'd have made it happen without you."

Weller gave him a look that said he was still listening.

"I'd wracked my brains, believe me. And nothing."

"Nothing."

"I mean, how do you go about calling off the dogs, when the dogs have been out there barking for half your life? When you're the one who set them out there to begin with?"

"I don't know," said Weller. As if it were all none of his business.

"How do you tell people the world has changed, when you've been telling them over and over again that it never would? That change was impossible?"

Janey gave her head a shake. "So you're saying that you knew all along—"

"I am."

"—and you'd have told everybody the truth—"

"I would have."

"—if you could have just figured out a good way to put it."

"Correct."

"I don't buy it."

Oates shrugged like a man capable of accepting anything, like a man so secure in his own comprehension of the world that he can forgive any amount of unbelief on the part of those less enlightened. "I was desperate," he said. "All of these people depend on me, and I'd been telling them lies every single day."

"Whose fault was that?"

Oates cocked his head toward her. "I could blame it on Marlowe," he said, "but that wouldn't be entirely fair, would it? I could say that I was only doing as I was told, when the truth is that I should have been man enough to stand on my own two feet."

"I saw Marlowe," said Janey. "He wasn't in any shape to be giving out orders."

"The colonel went up and down. He had his good days and his bad days."

"I'll bet."

"I felt an obligation to him."

Janey's look said that Oates hadn't been following anybody's orders but his own.

Oates understood. "You're entitled to your point of view," he said.

"Point of view doesn't have anything to do with it."

Janey, said Weller. Not exactly calling her off, but letting her know that there were limits. Limits to judgment and to hospitality and to patience.

"Now, Henry," said Oates, "let her go on. Let her have her say." Suggesting an understanding between the two men that had never existed and never would. "It's always best to get these differences out in the open. Clear the air. Right?"

Weller couldn't help himself. "I don't remember you as the kind of fellow who wanted to give anybody a fair hearing."

"People change," said Oates. "And circumstances change, too." He clapped both of them on the back like the oldest of friends or the most trusted of conspirators, and then he turned them around and indicated the feast that was about to begin. "There'll be plenty of time to explain everything. In the meanwhile, let's eat."

*

It was all hands on deck in Spartanburg these days, and because there was so much work the travelers fit right in. Their labor and their insight were welcome in equal parts. They were well fed by way of reward, and they gave back without hesitation.

Coming as they did from the Northeastern Empowerment Zone, where the growing season was short and resources were scarce, they knew some things about working the earth that people accustomed to living in the hothouse environment of the car factory didn't. They'd learned to be careful with what they had, particularly water and fertilizer and anything whatsoever that might somehow be prodded into germination, and they were happy to share what they knew—even though at the outset they couldn't imagine teaching anything to people capable of raising such crops as they had already feasted upon.

The new children, Penny included, entered into the routines of the school. Each morning groups of five and six passed down the same lamplit streets as usual, through the quiet residential neighborhood and the adjacent district of shops and workrooms, but now when they came to the old ball field they found themselves no longer in the roofed-over dark but practically out in the open, with cool fresh air and warm bright sunlight streaming toward them from the loading docks to the east where the farming crews had already lifted the doors. It felt to them—even to the youngest; perhaps especially to the youngest—that they were on the verge of something precipitous. That the world as they had known it was vanishing forever, diminishing behind them like memory or landscape, to be replaced by some new reality that was larger and more permanent.

Weller took Liz beyond the walls of the car factory in search of power. Not the kind that Oates possessed, which was a power that constrained things, but the other kind—the kind that turned things loose. People here had been burning pretty much everything they produced in the way of unrecoverable trash since the beginning, and they'd taken advantage of it to generate a certain amount of electricity, but there was always a need for more and now that need was going to grow. They'd done well enough, considering that the core founding group had been a team of Black Rose discontents, former Navy SEALS and Special Ops guys who'd committed themselves to following Marlowe wherever he went—survivalists and fighting men, not a real engineering type among them—but they'd have to do better now. They'd have to look outside their own limitations, their own closed universe, and draw on other resources as yet undiscovered. Weller was the man for that kind of work. He'd performed exactly this kind of magic before, once for his own purposes and later for Patel's tobacco station. "What we're looking for," he told Liz as they climbed a ladder to the roof, "is a hill that doesn't seem to fit into the landscape. We'll know it when we see it." And sure enough they did, pay dirt in this case being a municipal landfill where old Spartanburg—the original city, long abandoned—had for generations buried its refuse. It was a natural gas well now, at least to someone like Weller who knew what he was looking for. All he needed was a handful of strong backs and a half-mile of iron pipe, which was easily salvageable from that hurricane fence they'd taken down.

As for Janey, she went right back to her old job in the machine shop. It didn't suit her, though. Not anymore. Not now that she'd seen the world.

Bud came by to see her one morning, and he found her in the outer doorway looking off into the distance. She had a look of yearning and inquiry and he took advantage of it. "That's where I'm bound," he said.

"Where, exactly?"

"Anyplace. Anyplace but here."

"Lucky you."

Janey sighed. "In my case, those days are over."

"Not necessarily."

"Meaning?"

"Meaning you can always make a change."

"And run like you two?"

"I don't know. Maybe. Maybe something else."

"There isn't much else."

Janey's boss stepped away from his work and looked over in their direction. He cleared his throat a couple of times. The work day had begun and he didn't appreciate any kind of distraction, whether it was a visitor like Bud or the inspiration that Janey was seeking out there on the horizon. Janey looked at him and indicated her understanding by means of all she could muster in the way of a smile, and then she turned and looked back out the door one last time.

"Join the Navy and see the world," Bud said. It was something he'd read on a sign somewhere.

"What's that supposed to mean?"

"I don't know. Take things into your own hands, I guess."

*

In the evenings people went outside or what had once passed for outside, old habits dying hard the way old habits always do. They sat on their front porches under the high glass roof and they lit candles and they looked up at the stars. They drank lemonade or played cards or did both. Talked with one another across tables and from porch to porch. Electricity was rationed, and most of the rooms in the houses and the one apartment building were dark. It wouldn't be that way forever. Not once Weller finished piping in gas and setting up a bigger generator. People were already wondering aloud about what might happen then. Would these front porches become useless? Would families shut themselves away indoors?

Bud and McCall had a little apartment they were free to use for as long as they stayed around. It had belonged to a guy who'd gotten married and moved out just a couple of weeks before. It had one bedroom and one bed, which meant somebody used the couch, which meant Bud. He was shorter than McCall and the couch fit him better. He was fine with it. He was fine with the whole deal. The married guy had vacated the premises but he hadn't emptied them. Nobody emptied anything. He left the furniture and the dishes and the books and so forth, which made the place comfortable. The world was made of hand-me-downs and cast-offs anymore. This world, at least.

Days they took it easy and evenings they came out on the street with the rest, under the dim streetlamps and the high stars. Circulating from house to house as if they wanted to get to know everybody in town. Bud launching into conversations and asking questions and telling his life story or something resembling it to anyone who would listen. McCall hanging back the way he always did, keeping his own counsel.

Oates was always out there with the rest of them. He hadn't been before, and Marlowe hadn't even been seen in public for God knows how many years until they'd brought him out of his quarters in a pine box, but everything was changed now. Oates was out there every night, camped on a porch swing that hung from a pair of rusty chains and creaked as he rocked himself back and forth. That porch swing was his throne even though it didn't look it. It was the seat from which he heard everybody's stories and told them his own. Passed along holy writ. Bud and McCall gave him a wide berth, preferring to stick with common people who knew they were common.

Eleven:

Piedmont

Hutchinson headed south. The Humvee wouldn't keep going forever, but he had spare gas and plenty of extra rubber and he'd be content to walk when the time came. South made sense if only because no other direction did. North was civilization or what passed for it, and he'd had enough of civilization. West was too big and too dry. It was all a wasteland out there now, empty land and no one to need the things it had once grown. America's breadbasket without a crumb left in it.

So South it was. He had something of an affinity for the south. Growing up along the Mason Dixon he knew his parents had come from down there originally. From Georgia. They'd taken him there once or twice, before people stopped going anywhere for fun. They'd taken him to visit his grandparents in Atlanta. He remembered expecting water, but Atlanta wasn't anywhere near water. You'd think it would be, with a name like that.

He knew he'd never make it to Atlanta now, not on the gas he had even in reserve. Not with the mileage the Humvee got. But that was all right. His grandparents were long gone. Atlanta didn't have an ocean. You never even heard about Atlanta anymore. He was just heading south for somewhere to go.

*

The last thing he ever thought he'd see was a man on horseback. Correction. That was the *next to last* thing. The actual last thing was a whole troop of them, a dozen men and a dozen horses, spread out along a dry riverbed trending west to east from out of the Piedmont. Their destination was anyone's guess.

He was stopped on a ridgeline marked by high-tension towers whose broken lines hung loose and banged in the wind. From a distance they made a kind of musical sound, but up close it was a clanging that went straight down into the ground and made the earth vibrate. Kudzu muffled some of it. Kudzu was everywhere, great ropy vines that the Humvee passed beneath like jungle vegetation. The people on horseback may have been keeping an eye out, but they wouldn't have seen Hutchinson on account of the dense cover of green. He hadn't willfully kept out of sight, it was just something that his training saw to without his even having to pay attention. He was glad for it now, though. Even though the riders below didn't look especially vigilant, one of them might have looked up and seen him and what then.

Riders.

The word passed through his mind and set off a signal.

A generation or two prior, the word to have the same effect might have been *trolls* or *ogres* or *elves*. Words for things that in the end were just words, because the things themselves didn't exist. Not really.

And yet here they were.

Twelve:

The Lab

Dr. Patel heard rumors. People said there was a college not far away. A university. With laboratories and everything. Nobody had been there since the whole world shut down, but people still remembered. Now that the car factory doors had been sprung open, people's memories were coming back. Things they hadn't let themselves think about for years. How the commercial district around Spartanburg had sprawled out in the decades before the Great Dying. How there'd been places to buy anything you wanted and eat anything you were hungry for. How there'd been wall to wall cars on the highways and a decent airport halfway to Greenville where you could fly anyplace you wanted as long as you didn't mind changing planes in Charlotte. How there'd been state parks and county parks and just ordinary undeveloped tracts of land with lakes and streams where you could catch fish. Some of them were pay lakes, where the owner stocked the fish in the springtime and you just pulled them out for money. People wondered what those fish were like now, if there were fish at all. Maybe they'd all died or maybe they'd mutated into something else or maybe they were still just fish. People talked about stuff like that all the time now. The way things had been. It was as if the whole world had been restored to them just by the opening of a door they'd hardly even had the opportunity to step through.

The college, though. That was what interested Patel. She imagined what it would be like to be back in a proper lab again, whether it was up there or back here using equipment they'd haul down. Probably here, because here she'd have power. How far away was it, she wondered. Not more than fifteen miles, people said. Patel said you could do that in a day easily, and people looked at her surprised because she didn't look like the long-distance type. She'd put in some miles lately, though, that was for sure, and she wasn't afraid of much anymore.

*

Come Friday night the little diner was crowded. Six people were jammed into every four-top booth with a chair pulled up at the end for a seventh. Every stool at the counter was occupied, some of them double. Patel was at the end of one table, asking what anybody knew about the college. One woman said she'd been accepted there herself a long time ago. It was UNC. The University of North Carolina. She hadn't gone, because her family's money had run out fast toward the end and what good was an education anyhow when you had to be born into Management of Ownership if you wanted to get anyplace in life? Why waste your energy on a dead end?

One of the men said he could top that. He'd actually been enrolled there once, but he'd gone on a scholarship so he hadn't needed money. A basketball scholarship. They'd said if he played hard and kept his nose clean, he'd get a free education. Except it turned out that playing hard was more important than anything. More important than keeping his nose clean and more important than getting an education, and not just to himself but to everybody else involved. In the end he'd never made the pros and he'd never made anything of himself otherwise. He'd run out of motivation and then he'd run out of time. In other words he was still as dumb as he'd been the day he'd enrolled, and now it was too late. Ha ha ha.

Bud and Janey were sitting in the next booth, but thanks to the crowd everybody was part of the same conversation. "Why don't we go check it out tomorrow?" Bud asked her.

"UNC?"

"Get a little fresh air. Do you a world of good."

Janey's heart leapt, but she resisted. "I have a lot to do," she said. It was true, but not entirely. Work would wait until Monday. To be honest, she didn't know why she was saying it wouldn't. Maybe it was Bud himself.

Patel ended up changing her mind without half trying. "If you won't go," she said, "I will." That was all it took.

*

Bud had hoped to have Janey out there in the boondocks all by herself, get to know her a little better one on one and so forth, but it didn't turn out that way. Half a dozen more people showed up to keep them company, Patel included, although she hadn't planned on going at the start. Come morning she was right there with the rest of them, saying she hadn't been able to sleep all night for wondering about what they'd find. Saying she had to see it for herself.

McCall looked at the lot of them over breakfast and whispered to Bud that maybe he ought to start a little business here in Spartanburg. Tour guiding or something on that order.

Bud laughed.

McCall said no, he was serious. Maybe only halfway serious, but still. A person couldn't run forever. Plus Bud liked people, which was more than he could say for himself.

Bud said no, settling down wasn't in the cards.

McCall said all right, suit yourself. He said a person with the proper character attributes could be a regular Christopher Columbus around here, that was all. Discovering stuff that everybody else had forgotten about and collecting the glory.

*

It was amazing how slow these people were. Maybe because of how much they carried. Food and food and more food. Like they were going on a week-long picnic. To tell the whole truth it was a good thing they'd taken as much as they had, since as slow as they were they were going to be out for a while. Definitely overnight. That was fine with Bud, it meant more time with Janey, but it still drove him nuts.

So he went on ahead. He and Janey and Patel too, even though she was pretty old by comparison. She was plenty tough, though. Tough as nails, and determined. She didn't quit. You had to respect that, and he told her so. Told her he respected how she hadn't gone soft like these other people who'd spent their whole lives indoors. He'd never seen anything like them, except for maybe once. Never mind. He didn't want to talk about that.

They traveled in the usual way, mostly out of habit. They went stealthily, keeping a low profile and sticking to places where they couldn't be seen even though there probably wasn't anybody around to see. Not after the reputation that Spartanburg had developed. Bud knew that you could never be sure. There were people in places where you didn't expect them. People on the margins of civilization and people way the hell out in wastelands where you couldn't imagine how they scraped by. Some of those people were hardly even people anymore, if you wanted to be technical about it. They'd sprung from mutated genetic material, and they'd most likely keep on mutating as long as they kept on having babies. God knew where it would lead. Evolution in action. Survival not necessarily of the fittest but of the most desperate and resourceful.

In other words it didn't pay to be careless. Not out here. So he and Janey and Patel watched their step, keeping to the shadows of the big crumbling highways and overpasses. He couldn't speak for how the others behaved themselves, but it wasn't his problem.

The college turned out to be situated pretty much where the rumors had said it would be. Hardly any distance at all from Eighty-Five, although you wouldn't know it if you weren't looking for it. The place looked for all the world like the legend it had become with the passing of the years and the closing off of the world: ruined and stripped like everything else, its grassy quadrangles gone to weed and low brush and its brick buildings densely vine-covered. Every window was smashed, and doors gaped like mouths.

Patel stopped dead upon seeing it. The first time she'd stopped at all, to Bud's recollection. She froze and inhaled deeply and something in her collapsed. "Whatever they had here is gone now," she said.

But it wasn't entirely so.

*

The lab had escaped. Enough of it, anyhow. The key instruments, certain important gauges and tools. The gas lines that supplied the burners and ovens had been drained long ago, of course, and most of the glassware was gone. Scavengers had attacked the very sheetrock of the walls, splitting it open in great brutal gashes that showed where iron pipes and copper cabling had once run. The veins of the building, extracted for salvage. Patel didn't care about them, since there'd be no electrical or water supply to feed them anymore.

There were pipettes, though, and funnels and graduated cylinders and clamps and so forth. And that was just the small stuff. There was a spectrophotometer that looked to be in working order, and a colorimeter and various thermostats and temperature controllers that nobody had bothered taking. They'd been utter mysteries to whoever had ransacked this place, useless as cave paintings. And now, after all these years, they spoke to Patel in her own language.

"We have to get all this back to the factory," she said, and Bud figured it would take some time, which was one thing he had in dwindling supply. But if he could go back and forth with Janey, maybe it would be worth sticking around.

*

They made a thorough inventory on paper from a supply cabinet. Reams and reams of it, white as snow.

"They must have given up early," Patel said, "if they left all of this behind." The way she saw it, these reams of plain white paper contained the history of a world not yet lived and therefore not yet written down. The ineffable and inevitable future where anything could happen.

By the time they'd finished figuring out what they ought to take home it was late in the afternoon, very nearly evening, and even though Bud would have gone back in the dark if he were operating alone he suggested that they stay. Nobody objected. It was an adventure. An overnight out in the big old haunted world that was turning out not to be so haunted after all.

Still, when they'd loaded up the next day and trekked back to the car factory with everything they could carry, most of them were glad to be back home. Relieved and not exactly eager to venture out again. All but Bud and Janey, who volunteered to shuttle everything else back over the next little while. It might take a month or so if he was lucky. Breaking the big equipment down into pieces first rather than kill themselves or risk being anything other than adaptable out there in the unknown. If the dismantling got complicated they might need to spend nights away and Bud planned on doing exactly that whether it turned out to be strictly required or not. He wanted the opportunity to stay up half the night and look at the stars through the big busted plate glass windows of the lab and get to know Janey better in the way a man and a woman might get to know one another. To whatever extent it would be possible. You never knew.

He liked Janey. He told himself that it wasn't just a matter of short-term opportunity, but that the two of them might actually get something going if the opportunity presented itself. She wasn't any hothouse flower, that was for sure. Not like the rest of them. She had plenty of strength both physical and mental and she had an adventurous spirit and she'd sprung herself from the car factory only to find herself deposited right back where she'd started. The whole world out there and no way to access it—no reason to access it—beyond what Bud himself might offer her. That was the gift he could give to her. The gift of the whole wide world.

That and a running start on the hell that was about to break loose in the car factory—once he'd delivered a certain package that he'd been keeping to himself for a while now.

*

Bud had hidden the syringe. He and McCall were sharing an apartment for the time being, so he kept it under his mattress. McCall had seen the syringe previously, and he'd have recognized it right away if he'd happened upon it again, and that would have been the end of the whole deal.

It was McCall who'd first gotten wind that there was money to be made by planting a certain virus in the fertile ground of Marlowe's Retreat. It was McCall who'd made contact with Black Rose after they'd run across Weller and the rest, and McCall who'd made the deal, and McCall who'd had second thoughts just before they sealed it. McCall had always been a tougher negotiator than Bud, and he pretty generally cut whatever deals had to be cut, and he'd cut this one just the same until he decided not to follow through on it.

His change of heart hadn't altered anything for Bud, though. Not anything except the money situation, which it had improved. While McCall was putting together supper he'd had words with that fellow from Black Rose and told him he'd do the job himself. Do the job himself and keep all the money. He got half of it up front, right then and there.

Over the last few days there'd been small change of plans. Bud had decided that McCall, not some anonymous and unlucky local, would be the one to get the injection. That had never been an option until Bud began to think that McCall might double-cross him once they got back north. Tell Black Rose that he'd come to his senses and done the job with Bud. Tell Black Rose that the rest of the money should be his. It might not happen, but it might. And why take the chance? Besides, there was no way Janey would leave Spartanburg with both of them. No way McCall would let it happen and probably no way that Janey would either. With no more McCall, Bud would need a partner and Janey could be it.

There were a few things they still needed to collect from the lab. They'd been going back and forth from time to time for weeks now, as Patel found one thing or another on her inventory sheet that she just had to have. They had another trip to run tomorrow. And if the virus worked as fast as Black Rose said it did, an outbreak here would be just the thing to pry Janey loose for good.

He did it in the middle of the night. Pulled back McCall's bedsheet a little bit and slid the needle into the big muscle of his thigh. The needle so impossibly thin that McCall, accustomed to sleeping in the wild with every sense on the alert, didn't even stir.

Thirteen:

Weller's Retreat

Weller worked hard at fitting back in. He reported every morning to the machine shop, taking up the same tools and the same jobs in the same bay he'd occupied when he was here under what you could describe as false pretenses. When Oates had him working like an indentured servant, toward a goal that he'd kept drawing farther and farther out of reach. Those were the days when he'd gotten to know Janey by day and labored at finding and fixing up the X9 by night.

He felt older than that now. And not by just a few months.

He'd worked more or less around the clock back then, and he wasn't sure he could do it again now to save his soul. But back then he'd been doing it for Penny, and now he was just putting in time.

Still, keeping your head down had its advantages. If anything went wrong, it wasn't going to be his fault. He'd upended the world before, and he'd seen some benefits for it but he'd seen some troubles too. Mostly troubles. Things he hadn't expected. The death of that schoolteacher, for one thing. The destruction of Patel's outpost and the uprooting of all of her people. To say nothing of the uprooting of his own family. They'd never get back home. This was what they had now. This was what they had become. And the sooner he got accustomed to setting a good example for Penny and Liz, the better off they'd all be.

*

Janey wasn't in the shop much. Weller noticed her absence and hated himself for noticing. It wasn't about her, though. It was about what she'd gotten clearance to do. She and that Bud were out in the great big world making a difference. Scavenging parts for Dr. Patel's research and bringing them back and making something new possible.

They were out there, and he was in here.

He kept his head down, though, and concentrated on his work. Now that the farming operation had expanded into the acreage beyond the car factory, the machinery was taking a beating like never before. It was all he could do to keep up with the repairs. The rest of the crew was still mostly concentrating on little gas-powered transport ATVs and old beat-up trucks that they kept running, and on some in-place upgrade work on water and sewage pumps, so most of the farm equipment fell to him. Harrows with broken teeth and balers that got jammed and cultivators that wouldn't cultivate. He did the work, but he didn't find any of the usual joy in it.

Fourteen:

Riders

Riders were bogeymen.

Riders didn't exist.

Riders were pure myth, and they lived where myths always lived, in the darkness at the edge of the known world. According to the stories that every child heard growing up, and that every child rejected when he became an adult, they were the sort of half-human creature that any culture will sooner or later invent to keep its weakest and most impressionable from getting any big ideas.

And yet here they were.

Everybody always said that Riders were to be feared. That they were lawless and bloodthirsty marauders who ranged freely in the untracked wastelands beyond the cities and beyond the Empowerment Zones, subject to no rule but their own. The conventional wisdom held that the only forces that kept the Riders from massing together and overwhelming ordinary mankind were their hatred of confinement and their vast capacity for bloodletting. Put three or four of them together in one place and wait any amount of time whatsoever and only one would emerge—and that single unfortunate would be staggering, bloody, wounded to the very margin of death.

The only sure way to kill a Rider, they said, was another Rider.

And yet here they were.

Hutchinson didn't know what to make of it.

He'd never even seen a *horse* before. Not a live one in the flesh, anyway. But now he stood alongside his Humvee watching a mounted line of them disappear down the green pass, searching his brain and trying to account for what he was witnessing. There'd never been any question in his mind about horses, any more than there'd been doubt about rabbits or mice or birds. They were in books and photographs everywhere. The landscape of White Washington was peppered with their marble likenesses, not the least of which was the twice-life-sized statue of President Cheney, the old Angler himself, mounted triumphantly upon the rampant back of his well-known favorite, Liberty.

But here were a dozen or more of them in the flesh, ridden by figures who could have grown out of their very backs to judge by how much at home they looked. They rode as if they'd been born there. Born to complete these four-legged creatures like something out of a myth even older.

What could he do? He gathered some essentials—rations for a few days' travel, body armor and a compass and a flashlight jammed into a rucksack—locked the Humvee up tight, and set out on the trail that the Riders had followed. He was drawn after them like a man in a dream. To his doom or to his salvation hardly mattered.

Doom he had coming, after what he'd let happen in Connecticut.

Salvation, on the other hand, would be an unmerited surprise.

*

There was blood on the trail here and there. The longer he walked and the more of it he saw the more regular it proved. A fat drop or two every eight or ten paces. The Riders hadn't been hurrying, though. Not by the look of them and not by their track. He didn't think they were tending to one of their number who'd been wounded or even to a wounded horse. He thought maybe they'd been hunting. He thought that one of them was most likely bearing some dead prize. A deer. An elk. God knew.

The old schoolyard song came back to him as he marched along the horse trail.

Once there was a little boy wouldn't say his prayers,

And when he went to bed at night away upstairs
His Mama heard him holler and his Daddy heard him bawl,
And when they turned the covers down, he wasn't there at all!
They sought him in the rafters and the closet and the chest,
They sought him in the kitchen and the attic and the rest,
And they sought him up the chimney flue and everywhere, I guess.
But all they ever found was his jammies strewn about,
And the Riders'll git YOU if you don't — watch — out!

It gave him a shiver. A grown man—not just a grown man, but as nearly a perfect a specimen of a grown man as ten hard years of Black Rose training could produce—and the old schoolyard song still made him shiver just the way it had twenty-five years ago. Back when he was a little boy who didn't know any better. Back before he'd put away childish things. It was funny, really. It was laughable, when you came down to it. The way your mind worked. But it was also a distraction from the mission at hand, a distraction that he dared not tolerate. He willed himself to concentrate his attention on the things that mattered. He pressed the song out of his head. He scanned the ridge lines for any sign of surveillance and he studied the tracks that went before him to see if any had turned off on some hidden side trail and he scolded himself for childishness and cowardice. But if the hairs on your neck want to stand up on their own, there's not much you can do about it.

The Riders'll git you if you don't watch out.

He stepped up his pace, hurrying toward whatever fate might lie ahead.

It was useless to think he might overtake the Riders or even keep pace with them, given that he was on foot. The horses were walking, picking their way carefully along the down-bound trail, but they were still horses. Horses changed everything. All at once the feeling came over him of being on the wrong side of history and evolution. The side that got bypassed and left behind. He imagined this world without transportation of any sort, just tribes of Red Indians minding their own business in their own territories, and then he imagined what must have happened when the first horses arrived. He thought they'd come from somewhere in Europe. One of those old countries they had over there, like Italy or Spain. Those first horses made a whole different world possible. You could quit minding your own business if you had horses. You could go mind somebody else's business instead. You could travel a great distance to raid their villages and take their scalps and rape their women and murder their children. Steal their belongings and claim their territory for your own.

Horses, it seemed to Hutchinson as he made his way down the trail in the fading light, had sparked the invention of the modern world. A chain of violent struggle, at the top of which he had existed for a little while. But not anymore.

*

They had built themselves a village from scratch. Of course—and why not? Hutchinson couldn't see a band of Riders ever making use of some town left behind by ordinary men. They would never be scavengers of that low sort, taking the shell of the old world and fitting themselves into its contours. They'd be above that. Part of him knew how ridiculous it was to think that way—drawing conclusions not from observed reality but from beliefs and prejudices and fears born in childhood—but he thought that way anyhow. And so he wasn't surprised when he came upon their rough-hewn village in the foothills.

It was nearly invisible, and at the same time it was plain as day. Just another part of the landscape and made of the same materials. Rocks and trees and grass. Wood with the bark still on. Everything fitted together as if it had grown up that way out of the dirt a long time ago, maybe before man had set foot on this earth. The only thing that looked worked on was a big open paddock cut from the trees and fenced in. It was grassy, though, and contoured to the falling land, and even that could have almost happened by itself.

When he first caught sight of the settlement, the light was filtering sideways and the sun was barely up. He'd been walking for only a little while, and he was glad that he'd stopped when he had the night before or else he'd have wandered right into the middle of them. He was glad he'd

had no fire, either, although he never made a fire. That was standard operating procedure. Some principles still held.

The Riders made fire, though. He saw smoke rising up here and there,
from chimneys and from fire circles. He saw people moving about. He took
one last look and left the path and followed a little game trail up into the
woods, and then he left the game trail and went farther on, moving slowly
and carefully, treading deeper into the forest and aiming for a little outcropping he'd seen. He didn't go all the way to the outcropping but he drew
close to it. There was a fire circle there too. Old and loosely built and
probably used only occasionally. Probably made by kids. Kids were the
same everywhere, he guessed. There was no sign of horses up here so they
must have come on foot when they came. He could imagine them gathering up here nights, looking down on the world of their parents, itching for
something else the way every kid does.

He sniffed the air and stayed in the woods, sinking back just deep
enough that he could see out but not be seen. He waited until the wind
picked up and began to toss the branches of the trees along the ridgeline,
and then he climbed.

Fifteen:

Viral

Penny cried out in her sleep, tearing the night in half. Liz ran in and found her twitching in the bed like something hooked up to an electrical current. Like she was made of nothing but nerves and every one of them was firing. Her eyes were pushed wide open in the half-light from the hall and they were rolled back in their sockets, whites showing, as if something within her didn't want to see. Wanted to stop seeing altogether now that she'd begun.

Liz went right back in time the way a mother will, right back to that night underneath the apple trees somewhere in what was once Pennsylvania, where her poor child had first done something like this. Like this but not to this degree. The nervous twitching and the electrical impulses gone crazy but not the crying out and not the rolling back of her eyes in their sockets.

"He's bleeding," Penny said. "Make him stop bleeding."

Her mother quickly checked the bedclothes, the way a mother does, just in case. Nothing.

"He's bleeding."

Liz sat and put her arms around the child, thinking to wake her slowly through the gentle force of her own insistent embrace. The child still shaking, still looking nowhere. The mother whispering, "Now, Penny. Now, Penny."

"He won't stop bleeding."

"It's all right, Penny." Rocking the child as if she were a year or two old, not five years old and almost ready to turn six.

"He won't stop. You can't make him stop."

"Nobody's bleeding, Penny. It was a bad dream. Everything's fine." Looking down at the child in the half-light and making eye contact this time. Penny beginning to look like herself again. Lying stilled in her mother's arms and starting to look like herself again except terrified.

"Yes he is," said the child. "He's bleeding but you can't see it."

"Because it was a dream." She started to hum an old lullaby, something she hadn't thought of in years but that came right back without so much as a thought.

Penny sat up. She shook herself free of her mother's grasp as if to assert her full consciousness and to reinforce the import of what was about to come. "No," she said, "it wasn't a dream. You can't see it because it's inside. *He's bleeding inside."*

*

At some point her father rose from his bed and came to stand in the doorway. Just his outline there against the dim light from the hall. Penny grew quiet and closed her eyes, and Liz looked at Weller and raised her shoulders for an instant and let them down again. *One of those things.* Some problems don't have answers and some, at least by the light of day, aren't even problems at all. Weller shrugged too. Not so long ago he would have been the one comforting Penny, but ever since he'd left her with Liz in the hospital in New York City things had gone back to normal in that department. He missed it. He missed how he'd disrupted the natural order by taking her on that adventure they'd had together and he missed the sense he'd developed then that her fate and her future were one hundred percent in his hands. The responsibility he'd taken on and ultimately fulfilled, whatever else had happened in the process.

The poor child had been going blind, and he'd seen to it that she got better.

He practically longed for the time when forces of all kinds had been arrayed against him. When Anderson Carmichael and General Bainbridge had tried their best to bring him down. When those primitive and speech-less monsters in Greensboro had held him captive. When Major Oates had plotted against him and it had taken all of his skill and patience to bust out of this place.

Major Oates. What a laugh. The old man didn't even notice him any-more. Beneath notice was a strange place to be, after everything he'd done.

Liz was humming softly to Penny and Penny was sleeping again or almost. Weller took half a step into the room but Liz stopped him with the lift of one eyebrow. *No. Not now. She's finally resting.*

*

"It wasn't a dream," Penny told her mother in the morning. She was work-ing on a plate of scrambled eggs and toast. Her father was long gone, al-ready at his post in the machine shop.

"Of course it was."

"No. It was something I saw."

"Where did you see it then, if it wasn't in a dream."

Penny didn't answer. She had her mouth full and was busy with both hands, parceling out the bright yellow eggs onto squares of buttered toast.

Her mother didn't press. She leaned back against the sink and watched her daughter eat. Fresh eggs and real butter and toast that tasted like the wheat it had come from instead of like ashes. It seemed ungracious to press in the context of such things. Penny was just a child, anyway. She didn't know how the world worked, and she was making distinctions that didn't exist.

Besides, she seemed perfectly fine now. All better.

When the doors began to slam open all along the little neighborhood street and the children began to emerge onto their porches with their schoolbooks clutched under their arms, Penny leapt up from her chair and gathered up her own things and headed for the door. Stopping only for a kiss and a hug from her mother, who would wash the dishes before setting out into the newly tilled fields. That was something she knew about. Farm work was farm work, even though the results here were incalculably better than back home in Connecticut.

Back home was beginning to sound funny to her ears.

Maybe this would be home after all.

*

The virus worked fast. The first day McCall stayed home from work, and the second he was coughing up blood and bursting out in bruises all over every inch of his body. Hardly able to get out of bed to go see the medic but forcing himself. He wondered where in hell Bud was, and then he knew. He knew not because of the symptoms alone but because there was a little painful prick mark in his thigh that a spider might have left. The damage was done. And Bud had gotten the hell out, no question about that. He would never come back. Not to a sinking ship.

McCall staggered down the stairs in the apartment building and set out for the infirmary. He didn't make it. He didn't even make it to the end of the street.

The old woman who found him face down on the sidewalk knew right away what it was. She'd lost both of her parents to it during the Great Dying and she would never forget. Witnessing the signs as they manifested themselves again on McCall's body brought everything back as if she had been orphaned only yesterday. His labored breathing and the paleness of his flesh with the dark bruises showing dimly through like something black rising up through calm water. His cracked lips and his reaching tongue and the agony upon his face.

She stepped back, and she screamed, and a dozen other people came running.

Nobody touched him. They all remembered that much.

Sixteen:

Gulliver

Hutchinson swatted away the first of them as if it were nothing more than a bug. Dimly aware of how quickly he'd gotten used to the presence of bugs. Singly and in little groups and in great swarms both visible and invisible, they were little marvels of biomechanics, persistent and aggravating and yet infinitely fragile. It seemed to him that if a person could get used to bugs, then a person could get used to anything. At least their stingers didn't seem capable of penetrating the Kevlar of his body armor.

The second one, though—thanks no doubt to a targeting correction on the part of whoever had taken aim and released the tiny thing into the still morning air—rose an inch or two above his collar and found its mark. The tiny needle entered his neck and the poison did its work with the next pulsing of his heart, and he was on his back in the leaf mold before he knew what had hit him.

He awoke surrounded, but not by adults. His captors were children. Working ropes around him and drawing them tight, rolling him onto a stretcher made of animal hide. He felt like a giant who'd crashed to earth from the top of some beanstalk.

The children were strong and skilled. They were a mixed group of girls and boys, the oldest certainly no more than ten or eleven, and he may as well have been being handled by a well-disciplined team of grown men. They'd gagged him with a length of rag but left his eyes uncovered so that he could see what was going on but couldn't make any complaint. He'd been dealt with far more clumsily by his own squads during various Black Rose rescue drills. *Rescue from what,* he wondered now. There'd been no power in the known world that would have dared confront Black Rose. But now his version of the known world had expanded to include not just Riders but the children of Riders, tough and skillful creatures of the wild, capable of who knows what. And as for rescue, he had only himself to rely on.

The prick where the dart had penetrated his skin still smarted, and he had a tingling in his extremities and the beginnings of a headache, but other than that he felt all right. He couldn't free his wrist to see exactly how much time had passed, but it didn't seem like much. The sun wasn't yet fully overhead. Whatever had been in the dart had worked fast and then dissipated just as rapidly.

He heard the whinnying of a horse somewhere off to one side and he craned his neck to see it but he was bound up so tightly all over that he couldn't move even that much. One of the children watched him try and smiled down at him with undisguised satisfaction. It wasn't a feral look. This child wasn't some wild thing operating according to instinct or just making up its own rules as it went along. The look it gave was a look that came from the accomplishment of a job well done, a look that anticipated praise for that job from some higher authority. Hutchinson knew that look well. He had seen it many times before in young recruits making their passage through boot camp. Seeing it now reinforced the idea that these children were being trained for something. Someone had taught them to hunt silently together in the woods, to use and perhaps even to manufacture the darts that had brought him down, to tie the complex knots that had bound him swiftly and securely to the stretcher. He figured that soon he would pass from the care of these children to the care of whoever had trained them, and he wondered what lesson they would take up next.

*

The children roped the stretcher behind the horse and set out for the village. There was a path nearer to the edge of the ridgeline that he hadn't noticed on his way up here, an open path nearly free of rocks and roots along which the horse dragged him. He'd have seen it earlier if he'd come out that far into the open and risked being spotted himself, but he'd stayed within the cover of the trees instead. Caution had cost him.

As they drew nearer to the village he smelled smoke. He couldn't see much of anything. Sky, mainly. Sky above with clouds moving way up and trees moving below. There weren't many rocks in the trail but he felt every one of them with the back of his skull since he couldn't raise his head. His backpack lay heavy on his chest but it didn't tumble off because the children had lashed that down too. Every now and then one of their number, probably one of the younger ones, would poke his shoulder with a stick and the others would hurry to make the troublemaker stop. There was no professionalism in poking your captive with a stick.

He noticed that they spoke English, and it struck him as strange. He didn't know what else they would have spoken. It wasn't as if they'd had generations to develop something new. Regardless, they didn't say much. They kept pretty quiet. Even the horse stepped lightly. That's what had let them sneak up on him in the first place. Sneak up on him and put a dart in his neck while he thought he was reconnoitering the village down below. He hadn't even had a chance to register much of whatever had been going on down there, they'd been on him so quickly.

Training. You just couldn't beat it.

The trail gradually flattened out and the smell of smoke slowly resolved into the smell of meat cooking. The cover of the trees grew more dense for a while and then it opened up as they emerged from the woods into the village proper. There were sounds of work everywhere. The hushed gravelly scrape of something other than himself being dragged. Regular hammering and sawing in rhythms that sounded nearly musical. He listened because listening was all he could do, but also because the sounds awakened something in him. He felt the weight of his pack on his chest and thought of the things it contained. The rations and the other supplies for a few days in the woods. He'd thought he'd been traveling light, but he saw now that he hadn't. He'd been traveling with the burden of an entire way of life upon his back. He'd been traveling according to the rules of the place he'd come from, not according to the rules of the place he'd been going. That had been his first mistake.

These people—call them Riders or call them whatever else you might want to call them—had established for themselves a culture that suited their place in the world. It called for work, hard work and lots of it, to the point where the work they did probably had no detectable end or even pause. They didn't have the luxury of loading up a regulation Black Rose backpack with regulation Black Rose rations and purifying the water in their regulation Black Rose canteen with regulation Black Rose iodine tablets.

Out here, it occurred to Hutchinson in one great momentary flash, his strength had made him weak. Weak enough to have been captured by a band of children. He decided that whatever lesson the universe was in the process of teaching him was one he'd get in spades.

*

Hutchinson's stomach was growling, and not because he was hungry. It was because of the overwhelming smell of cooking that filled the air. He'd been living on MREs for days now, and here was the insistent and pervasive scent of real food. It awakened systems within him over which he had no control. The children took him to a spot midway along the main line of buildings—he saw the foundations from the corner of his eye, and recognized the place from what little recon he'd accomplished from his perch in the tree—and then they untied the drag rope and set the horse free. One of them led it off in the direction of the grassy paddock but the rest remained, arranging themselves in a half-circle before Hutchinson, who lay on the ground like something discarded, one arm and one leg pressed up against a stone foundation.

For the longest time nothing happened. Someone was being taught patience, he decided. The children or else their prisoner. Maybe all of them. He'd done it to recruits himself, and he reconciled himself to this being his turn on the receiving end.

From where he lay he could only see upward. Upward along the neatly stacked wall of the log building and upward to the thatched roof that hung over the edge of it, along the margin of which the sun slowly inched. The day grew warm. He closed his eyes against the light. His guards grew restless, shuffling their feet and sighing, revealing themselves by these small measures to be at bottom just ordinary little children getting antsy to run off and do whatever.

And still they all waited. Until footsteps approached and a shadow crossed Hutchinson's vision and his guards snapped to attention.

"Up," said a woman's voice. "Lift him up."

"He's too heavy."

"Lift him up, I said. Find a way."

And the woman was gone again, along with Hutchinson's hope that this day had been on the verge of revealing its true colors.

It took a lot more rope, and it took the return of the horse, and it took a bumpy ride over to a tall barn that had a primitive block and tackle mounted to an arm high above its hayloft door, but the children lifted him up. It also took a certain amount of complaint, the children having continued reverting to something more like their natural selves now that they were safely back home. If Hutchinson hadn't been gagged, he'd have laughed out loud to hear these little imps calling the woman names that he'd surely been called many times himself. *Hard-ass* and *slavedriver* and worse. By the time they had him fully upright and propped up in the shadowy recess just inside the barn door, he was beginning to feel a kinship with her.

"Well done," she said when she returned. She drew near and reached into her belt and drew out a long curved knife that looked brutally sharp, but she didn't do anything with it right away. She just touched the flat of her thumb against its edge and gave it a couple of quick strokes across her thigh. Leather trousers—buckskin, probably. They'd be tough and durable and well-suited to riding through brush. The children were dressed the same way. It may as well have been a uniform, but it wasn't. It was just the uniformity of limited resources and unchanging needs.

He took the best look around he could, and decided that he'd been right about the buckskin. There were clearly deer in these hills, and the Riders were clearly well-practiced in making use of them. The carcass of one hung from a tripod alongside the barn. Another was roasting on a spit in the center of the green. Tanned skins were drying in the sun, stretched out on big wooden frames.

The woman stepped forward and raised the knife. She drew it close to Hutchinson's face and stopped, looking into his eyes. He didn't give her the satisfaction of responding. He blinked once on account of the smoke, but that was it. With a certain amount of care she worked the end of the curved blade beneath the rag that the children had used to gag him, but before she pulled back on it she stopped again. Knowing he wouldn't dare move a muscle.

She turned and addressed the children. "Where did you find him, anyhow?"

"On the big white rock," said one, pointing.

"Near the fire pit," clarified another one.

"Way up in a tree," a third explained.

"Way, way up," clarified one more.

"That'll do," said the woman. "Well done." Then she yanked back on the knife, effortlessly slicing through the rag and freeing Hutchinson to speak for himself if he dared.

*

"You taught them pretty well," he said.

The woman nodded. "They did fine. And to think we usually bring down nothing but game."

"Game," Hutchinson repeated, smiling. "What does that make me, do you suppose?" He said it without concern and without challenge. As if it were just an idle question.

She thought for a minute. "It makes you unlucky," she said at last. She bent and lifted his pack from where it lay in the dirt. Lifted the flap and looked inside, and then knelt down and started to spill out the contents.

"Careful," said Hutchinson.

"Careful of what."

"There's a pistol in there you don't want going off. Not with kids around." Maybe there was something maternal in her that he could work on.

She slid the knife back into her belt and located the pistol and held it up.

"At least the safety's on," he said.

"You weren't very well prepared, were you?" She studied the gun and flipped the safety off again, as if she'd done it a million times.

"I suppose not. I wasn't looking for trouble."

But she wasn't listening. She was burrowing into the pack with her free hand, sorting through what she found in its depths and pulling out this and that. A compass in a machined steel case. A first-aid kit. Boxed rations. She laid them out in front of the pack and pointed to them one after the other with the barrel of the gun. "Do you see what I see, children?"

One of the older ones took a step back.

Another one saw him go and followed suit, looking from the gear on the dirt to Hutchinson and back again as if he were confirming evidence of a ghostly visitation.

"What do you see?" said the woman.

The one who'd stepped back first whispered, *"Black Rose."*

At the sound of those two terrible words, the children scrambled away. The boy who had spoken, though, stood his ground. Hutchinson was still bound up tight after all. The child eyed him and drew himself up a little taller, suggesting either that he still felt some superiority to his captive or that he was all at once doubly proud of what his little band had accomplished. Probably both.

The woman laughed. "Fairy tales can come true," she said.

Seventeen:

Rumors

The medics had access to no higher authority than the treasured Black Rose Field Manual, and the Field Manual was silent as to the virus that had so quickly overwhelmed McCall. They fell back on the usual, bed rest and pain relief and plenty of fluids, even though the usual wasn't going to do him any good and they knew it. The virus had taken down most of what was left in the world outside the urban compounds of Ownership and Management back during the bad old days of the Great Dying, ravaging suburbs and towns and villages until it had finally burned itself out against whatever natural immunity certain individuals had been able to muster against it. There was no cure and there was no preventive mechanism beyond isolation. Happily for Ownership and Management, of course, isolation was something that they had in great abundance. Isolation was their specialty.

The medics hadn't even moved McCall out of the examining room. They'd just sealed the unit up around him and scrubbed themselves clean and hoped for the best. Protocols sprang up based on superstition and vaguely remembered folk wisdom and certain principles of cleanliness that went all the way back to Joseph Lister. One day went by and then another, and although McCall continued to deteriorate no one else seemed to show any symptoms.

Rumors spread, though. Faster than any contagion, since there was little to impede their movement. Most of the talk was among the natives.

The outsiders didn't hear much, because most of the rumors were about them. How they'd brought the virus to Spartanburg from elsewhere. How they either did or did not know what it was that they had done.

One of the other men in the machine shop, an old-timer who probably wasn't long for this world anyhow, let it slip to Weller over lunch. "I don't happen to believe what folks are saying about that kid of yours," he said. "Just so you know."

Mention of Penny instantly focused Weller's attention. "What do you mean?"

"People talk."

"Not to me they don't."

The old-timer took a slow bite of his sandwich. "You ain't heard?"

"I haven't heard."

The old-timer kept on chewing.

"What're they saying?"

"I don't give it no credence."

"Tell me anyhow."

"They say she brung it."

"The virus."

"They say somebody give it to her in the hospital, and then they turned her loose to get the rest of us."

"That's crazy."

"I think so."

"If they'd given her the virus, she wouldn't be here now."

"People say it was some special breed they give her. You carry it, but you can't get it."

"Then why didn't I get sick? Why didn't her mother?"

The old-timer just shook his head.

"Why didn't everybody we came with get sick?"

"Don't ask me."

*

Dr. Patel was the one who put it to rest. Science had never been an important discipline at Marlowe's Retreat. They had medics and they had a couple of electrical engineers and at the beginning they had had one Covert Ops specialist who knew about explosives and wiring and underwater demolition, but that was about the extent of it in the science department. Even the Covert Ops guy was long gone; the story was that he'd been out on recon with Marlowe one day and gotten killed by something that Marlowe himself had only barely escaped. No one had questioned the truth of it, and now it was all so long ago that even though the stories about cannibalistic mutant half-men and rampaging not-quite-dead walking corpses had been exposed for the fictions they had been all along, everybody had pretty well forgotten about the Covert Ops guy. Nobody even wondered what his real fate might have been. And now that Marlowe was dead, it was possible that nobody knew.

Regardless, science had never been big around Marlowe's Retreat—and because of that, Dr. Patel represented something utterly foreign. Old knowledge, brought back to life. The lost, now found. Her laboratory, set up in Marlowe's old quarters above the Town Office, had all of the qualities of an alchemist's lair. The windows glowed night and day with the pale light of data streams creeping across displays, and the air was forever punctuated with the sounds of precision machinery running itself. To judge from the constant level of activity, Patel never slept, unless perhaps she had engineered a duplicate of herself to carry out her work when the original needed some time off. Anything could have happened. Anything was possible. The line between doctor and witch doctor, if it had ever existed at all, had been obliterated.

And so when Weller heard the rumor about Penny—that she'd brought the virus that was killing McCall and would go on to kill every one of them if it had the chance—he went straight to Patel. He didn't go for the answer, since he already knew the answer. He went for reinforcement. "That's absurd," she said, hardly even looking up from her workbench. "I hope you straightened out whoever's been spreading these ridiculous stories."

"I can't straighten everybody out. Who'd believe me, anyhow? I've got a vested interest, don't forget."

"You've got credibility, too. Maybe more than you know."

"Not enough. Not enough to offset being her father."

She sniffed. "You underestimate yourself, Henry. That's not like you."

"I'm just being reasonable."

"You weren't being reasonable when you carried that child to New York in the first place."

"That was different."

"It was a fool's errand and you knew it."

"I didn't know it. I know it now, but I didn't know it then."

She looked up. "So you're asking me to lend you an air of authority."

"I'm asking you to *be* the authority. Talk to Oates. Have him spread the word."

"Oates says he isn't in charge anymore." She said it with a little smile.

Weller laughed out loud. *"Now* who's being unreasonable? Those overalls of his don't make him just another working stiff, and you know it."

"I do."

So she went, but only after making Weller promise he'd stay in the lab and mind some ongoing experiments until she returned. There was nothing to it. She assured him of that. Just watch this stream of numbers and turn this knob a notch if they went too far in either direction. Easy as pie.

*

Oates looked up and shaded his eyes with one hand. "To what do we owe the pleasure, Doctor?" He looked for all the world like the most ordinary hayseed type, wearing overalls and a sweat-stained baseball cap turned backwards. Actually chewing on a long green stalk of wheat from the indoor farms, leaning on the long handle of a hoe, and squinting at Patel. Just one of the crowd, except that everybody deferred to him and gave him room. Nobody quit working to interact with Patel except for Oates. They all kept their heads down, pretending not to listen. They all knew what was what.

Patel was fine with people listening in. The more folks who heard the truth from her mouth, the better. "Word's been getting around," she said, "that little Penny Weller brought the virus here from New York."

Oates gave her a look of practiced innocence. "Is it? Really? I hadn't heard."

Patel wasn't buying, but she didn't push it. "Hmm," she said. "I'd have thought—"

"Penny?" Oates asked, cocking his head. "From New York?"

"Yes. Some story about Ownership loading her up with a modified strain and sending her out into the world."

Oates chewed on that for a minute. "I suppose it makes sense."

"No," she said. "It doesn't make sense. It doesn't make any sense at all."

"I wouldn't be so certain. I can definitely see why they'd do it."

"They wouldn't do it. They wouldn't and they couldn't."

"Weaponizing a child and sending her out..." He nodded and looked into the distance, like a man whose mind was taking flight. "It's brilliant, don't you think? Brilliant in a terrible way, but brilliant all the same."

"It's anything but brilliant," she said. "It's pointless and impossible." She held up two fingers. *"Impossible,"* she said, bending her forefinger back, "because they don't have the technology for handling such a strain, to say nothing of creating it. They never did, and they never will." She bent back a second finger, going on like the academic she was. "It's *pointless,* because they'd never risk setting something like that loose. Why on earth would they want to kill untold numbers of their customers and their workforce? Where would PharmAgra be without those fields full of cheap labor? Not just cheap, mind you: they don't even pay people with actual money, just corporate scrip."

All around her, people shifted their heads by only the slightest and least perceptible angle. Listening in.

"You might have a point," Oates admitted.

"I used to work for those people, remember. They're vicious and they're greedy and there isn't a single moral fiber in a boardroom full of them, but they're not stupid."

"I'm not saying they wanted to start another Great Dying. I'm saying they wanted to eliminate us in particular. The people of Spartanburg. Their age-old enemies in Marlowe's Retreat."

It seemed to Patel that for a man who'd claimed ignorance a moment or two earlier, he'd thought this through pretty completely. Not completely enough, though. There were things he hadn't accounted for. "They didn't know Penny would even come here," she said.

He wasn't listening. "They've tried to exterminate us any number of times, you know. We've brought down their helicopters."

"They'd have expected her to go to straight home."

"Their strategists operate at an extremely high level," he said. "You may have worked for PharmAgra, but I worked for Black Rose. I know how they think. And believe me, it takes someone with my training to outmaneuver them."

All around, heads nodded.

"You have quite an imagination," Dr. Patel said.

All around, though, people began to whisper. And they watched her leave as if they were watching the disappearance of something rare and almost holy.

*

"That rumor?" Patel said when she came back to the lab. "Oates is the one who started it."

"Why would he do that?"

"He wants things back to normal. By blaming Penny, he thinks he can get rid of us. Put some fear back into people. Return things to the way they were before we arrived."

"He's a piece of work."

"He learns fast, I have to give him that. You said he ran this place from the top down before, and now he's had to figure out how to run it from the bottom up. A person in that position can't risk much in the way of competition—from you, from me, from anybody. He's conservative by nature. He doesn't like change. He wants everything nice and familiar."

"You think *he* gave McCall the virus? Just to get rid of us?"

"Now you're using your head," said Patel. "But no. It's a million miles beyond him. Plus he wouldn't risk infecting his own people." She tapped at a dial and studied some numbers that streamed across a blue screen. "The virus came from wherever it came from, and he was just taking advantage of it." Satisfied with what she'd seen on the display, she turned back to Weller with a smile so big that it startled him.

"What?" he said. He had never seen her look quite so happy.

"We're getting somewhere. It happened on your watch, Henry. If I were writing this up for the journals, I might have to make you my co-author."

"Co-author of what? What're you working on?"

"The virus. Once PharmAgra, always PharmAgra."

"But starting from scratch? Now we're talking impossible."

"Not from scratch. There were always rumors as to where the virus came from. More than rumors, really. There were actual reports, secret reports, that an interested party like me could get her hands on if she knew the right people."

"And *you* knew the right people."

"You bet I knew the right people. I worked alongside them until they didn't need me anymore. Or until they thought they didn't."

"You had theories."

"I did. And I still do. Plus I've got some decent analytical gear. Now all I need is a sample of McCall's blood."

Eighteen:

The Barn

One of the youngest kids spoke first: "My mama said Black Rose'd get me if I didn't behave."

The oldest poked him in the ribs. "I guess you've been plenty bad, then."

"Not me," said the younger one, backing away from Hutchinson. "I wasn't bad. He didn't come for me." The poor child was barely holding back tears. Frightened to death of this thing they'd captured and tied up and brought home.

"He's just teasing you," the woman said. Still kneeling by Hutchinson's pack, she leaned and put her arm around the littlest kid and drew him close. Then, leveling at the offender a glare that would abide no disagreement, she said, "You're just teasing him, aren't you?"

"Yes ma'am," the oldest said. "To tell you the truth, I didn't think there was any such thing as Black Rose. I thought it was all just make-believe."

The woman let go of the little kid and spoke to Hutchinson. "You're not here after these children, are you?"

"No ma'am, I'm not."

She stood, and she drew nearer to Hutchinson where he stood bound against the wall, her tone changed. "Then what *are* you here for?"

"Curiosity."

She laughed. "You call it curiosity. I'd call it recon."

"No. Really. Nothing of the sort. I saw your hunting party coming down from the mountains. I couldn't believe my eyes. I had to see more." He was bound so tightly that his breath was coming hard, but after a moment he went on. "You think Black Rose is a legend around here? You should hear what people up north say about Riders."

"Riders?"

"That's what they call you. Because of your horses. Where I come from, nobody's seen a live horse in a generation."

"I'll bet you'd have a use for them, though." Having decided that she was onto him and onto his mission.

"I can't imagine. We've got cars and trucks. I left my Humvee up in the mountains when I came down."

Something passed across her eyes suggesting that she had no idea what he was talking about—the word *Humvee* must have sounded to her like a term for some kind of domesticated animal—but she didn't ask. Asking would have indicated a weakness in her position. "You left it behind with your team, then."

"I don't have a team."

"So you're a scout. Working alone."

"I'm not a scout."

"When will they expect you to report in?"

"I don't report in. I don't have anyone to report to."

"Of course you do."

"I'm not even Black Rose anymore."

"Really."

"Really. I quit all that. I walked away. I'm a free agent."

She bent down and picked up the rag from his mouth and jammed it between his teeth again. He could have spit it out, but he didn't. Not yet. "When you're ready to start talking sense," she said, "I'll be ready to listen." Then she gathered up his pack and the things from it, and stepped out into the yard. She must have given some tiny signal to the children, too, because they came together as one and drew the heavy barn door shut.

*

One of them came back. The oldest of them although not by any means the biggest, the kid who'd jumped back at first but then recovered. He let himself in through some other door that Hutchinson couldn't see from where they'd left him, creeping softly on moccasined feet and keeping to the shadows. The shadows were treacherous and unreliable, though, shot full of light that broke through every unchinked joint in the log walls, and the boy's silhouette was visible in spite of his best efforts.

Hutchinson cleared his throat and spoke. "Hey there, son." He was thirsty, and he was tired of standing up against the wall, and his voice came out in a rusty croak that made the boy's shadow jump a little. As if Hutchinson had proven himself capable of seeing in the dark, like the boogieman he might turn out to be after all.

"I ain't your son," the boy said.

"I know that. I'm just being neighborly."

"I ain't your neighbor."

"Suit yourself." The boy had moved away from the wall and leaned up against a squarish shape that Hutchinson had taken for a bale of hay, but it resolved itself now into something more like a desk. With the kid around for perspective, Hutchinson saw that there was a group of them, maybe a dozen or so altogether, arranged in rows. "So what is this place," he said, "a schoolhouse or something?"

"You could say that. Sometimes."

"What do they teach you here?"

"Teach you to do as you're told, for one thing. Like you shouldn't've spit that rag out after she put it in."

"I guess she won't be too happy when she finds out."

"She ain't happy now. Won't take much to make her unhappier. Never does."

"You sound like somebody who's had about enough of schooling," Hutchinson said.

"You got that right, mister."

Hutchinson smiled broadly, as if the boy could see him. "I understand," he said. "I was like you once."

"I'll bet you were." There was approval in the sound of his voice now. Approval and respect.

Hutchinson heard it. "You suppose you could get me a drink of water?" he asked.

"Yessir," said the boy.

"I realize your teacher won't like it."

"That's all right." The kid left the same invisible way he'd come in, and returned a few minutes later with water in a turned wooden cup. He took his wary time approaching, even though Hutchinson was lashed down tight.

"For Christ's sake," Hutchinson said, "if I could get loose, I'd get my own damned water."

The kid laughed and then stopped laughing. "Maybe you want me closer is all."

"I don't want you closer. All I want's a drink."

The kid just stood there. Waiting for something.

"Good thinking, though. I'll grant you that."

The kid stood up a little straighter.

Hutchinson nodded as best he could, given the circumstances. "Yes, sir. You can't be too careful. Good job, boy."

Satisfied, the kid came forward and lifted the cup.

*

The kid had to duck back into the shadows when his teacher showed up again. She threw the big door wide, flooding the barn with light, and she almost saw him as he slipped around the corner. But not quite. That pleased Hutchinson too—the stealth that the child possessed—and his smile let it show a little bit.

"Don't *you* look like the cat that swallowed the canary," she said.

"I don't mean to."

She assessed the ropes that still bound him. "Whatever you think you're up to, think again."

"I'm just waiting."

"For the cavalry, I guess."

Hutchinson didn't say anything. He just flattened out his smile into a thin line.

"For the cavalry to come rescue you."

"I can see why you'd think that. But no."

"Okay. Maybe they don't call it a cavalry anymore."

Hutchinson brightened. "They do, actually."

"You do."

"*They* do. Like I said, I'm not Black Rose anymore."

Now it was her turn to flatten what was left of a smile into something less.

"They don't have horses anymore," he went on, "but they still call it the *cavalry*. Old habits. Just so you know."

"Just so I know who it is who comes thundering over the horizon to your rescue."

"There won't be any rescue."

She shifted her weight, and he realized that she was carrying his pack. Carrying it but slinging it around now to open the flap and show its contents. "There's got to be a tracking device in here someplace, but I'll be frank: I can't find it."

"If there *were* something like that, it might just be in one of my pockets." Thinking maybe he smelled an opportunity here.

"It's not," she said.

"I wouldn't be so sure."

"The kids emptied them before they tied you up," she said.

Hutchinson sighed.

"Nice try, but you're not getting loose."

"You've taught them well."

"I do my best."

So Hutchinson was back at square one. "Look," he said, "it's like I told you. I'm a deserter. Black Rose can't track me. They wouldn't track me if they could."

She shook her head. "I'm the one who taught those kids everything they know, and you think I'll believe an idiotic lie provided you say it often enough."

"Tell you what," he said, indicating the pack by his glance. "Go ahead and destroy everything in there, Smash it all to bits if that makes you feel safer. It's no use to me."

"You mean that."

"I do."

She reached in and drew out a long grooved knife. "That's what I was afraid of," she said, dropping the pack and moving in a step closer.

*

For a second he thought she might be planning to cut him loose after all. But instead she pressed the tip of the triangular knife against his neck, about half an inch above his body armor. Right alongside the bulge of his Adam's apple.

"Not that side," he said. "The right. Your left."

She switched sides.

"Brands are always on the right."

She prodded with the tip of the knife.

"Good thing I keep that blade clean."

"Don't talk." After a minute she located something hard. A little knot, just beneath the surface. Now that she'd found it she saw that the skin was puckered a little bit right there. Scarred and toughened. She didn't know it—how could she?— but that was one thing that differentiated Black Rose from the rest of the Management class. Generally you were born Management, just the same way you were born Ownership. Your brand went in before you were so much as a day old. Installed by a team of plastic surgeons if you were Ownership, by a low-level trainee at your father's employer if you were Management. Black Rose brands were the only kind that got installed in adulthood.

Hutchinson's had been done by a field medic and it had healed up poorly, and shaving over the spot a million times with cold water and a dull razor had only made it worse. After all these years it still bled sometimes. In other words the thing served as a constant irritation, on the order of a tiny pebble in his shoe, and right now he realized that he'd be glad to be rid of it for good.

"There you go," he said as she prodded at the spot. "That's the ticket."

"Hold still," she said.

Hutchinson didn't have any choice in that area—he could barely flinch—but he appreciated the warning anyhow. No sense risking his carotid artery over a little trepidation. He did hope that she knew something about anatomy, though.

The knife broke the skin and went in smoothly, incrementally widening the incision after itself. Blood ran along the gutter and streamed down his neck and down her hand. It didn't bother the woman in the least. She came up on the brand from underneath and gave the knife a quarter-turn and levered the handle down toward his chest, and the brand came loose and slid free, emerging from the hole and moving down the blade on a little river of blood.

"That was easy," she said. Taking the brand between her fingers and dropping the knife, and then using the thumb of her freed hand to press the incision shut. The brand was a little square with metal prongs mounted on each side, with some tissue and blood clinging to them. "I take it these are antennas," she said.

"I suppose they could be," said Hutchinson. "That'd be a good guess."

She let go of his neck and bent down to pick up the knife again. With red blood coming once more down Hutchinson's neck she strode over to one of the wooden desks and set the brand down on it. Then she struck it over and over again with the butt of the knife handle, until the casing was crushed and a crack had burst open in the side and the two prongs had come loose.

"That ought to do it," Hutchinson said.

She came back and tied a rag around his neck, doubling it up over the wound. It still leaked a little blood, but not much.

"You're going to let me loose?" he said.

"I'm going to give you more time to think about telling me why you're here," she said. And that was that. She spun on her heel and headed out into the fading light, and she pulled the heavy barn door shut behind her.

*

Once Hutchinson's vision had adjusted again to the darkness, he saw the kid. He'd been there in the shadows all along, watching, and now he stood up and came tearing back to Hutchinson's side.

"Holy crap," he said.

"What?"

"You got some nerve."

"I didn't have much choice in the matter."

The kid stood shaking his head. "I mean, *Jesus.* You just let her do it. You just stood there and let her stick in that knife and cut you wide open."

"Not all that wide, I don't think."

"Still."

"I didn't see you coming to my rescue, sonny."

The kid gaped. "Rescue?"

"Sure. You'll bring me water all right, but let somebody try to cut my head off, and you don't lift a finger."

"Never mind that," said the kid. "You're way past rescue anyway. No brand, no rescue."

Hutchinson sighed. "Nobody listens to me," he said.

"Let's get lost," said the kid, picking up the triangular knife and starting to work on the ropes. "I got a feeling you can show me a whole lot more than that damn teacher ever could."

Nineteen:

Blood

If a person had seams, McCall would have been coming apart at them. He was losing blood in great quantities, losing it as if the blood had a will of its own and a desire to escape the confines of his wretched body, losing it the way a sinking ship loses rats.

The medics had his bed slanted like an autopsy table. They'd given up on using sheets a couple of days prior and now he lay on a rubber tarp that was meant to keep the blood off the mattress. He had bandages over most of his body and they'd given up changing those too. It was a hazard and a waste of resources. One of the medics kept apologizing to him for these failures of care and hygiene, but McCall didn't care. Bandages and fresh linens were the last things on his mind. Plus he understood their point of view. He wasn't one of their own. And there were limits to everything, even kindness.

He understood all of that through a haze of pain that never seemed as if it could get any worse but always did. The only thing that kept him going, the only thing that focused his mind and permitted him to soldier on through one day after another, was the hatred he felt for Bud. His old partner who'd turned on him. He lay on that slanted rubber tarp with the blood leaking out of him to saturate the old bandages and crust on the outsides of them and weigh him down with the sheer lumpy mass of everything that had escaped his skin, listening to the clock tick and watching the contents of a saline bag slowly empty itself into a vein that somehow hadn't collapsed yet, and his fury over Bud's betrayal of his trust and his confidence and his friendship burned on and on within his mind like a kind of unquenchable flame. Like a beacon that led him on despite everything.

He was awake then, when Weller came in. Awake and more or less alert, although part of his consciousness had drifted off to pursue a vision of the revenge that he would take upon his former partner should he ever make it out alive. Weller was wearing the makeshift hazmat suit that the medics put on before entering McCall's presence. He unbolted the two doors one after another and came in even more tentatively than the medics did. That indicated that he was somebody new, somebody who might have some aim other than the usual. McCall would have shied at that idea if he could have shied, but any movement hurt. Everything cost him. A man with less motivation might have hoped that this new individual in the isolation suit was here to put an end to him, to put him out of his misery. But McCall's spirit carried him forward, clinging to the possibility of recovery and fearing the intrusion of anyone who might mean him harm, thanks to his deathless fury toward Bud.

McCall looked at the clock. It was quarter past three. Nobody ever came in now. They came in at the top of the even-numbered hours. There was a call button clipped to the bed but that didn't work unless the time was maybe five minutes before or after one of their scheduled visits. McCall figured the medics had other jobs, other responsibilities, and they couldn't spend their whole day hanging around the infirmary, keeping a vigil over a dead man.

Weller approached the bed. He leaned over and smiled down at McCall through the plastic screen of his helmet. "Hey," he said, muffled.

McCall's eyes opened a little wider.

*

"How're you doing, McCall?" It was just something to say. How he was doing was obvious to anybody. Weller didn't expect an answer, but he got one.

It wasn't much. Just one syllable, spat from between parched lips. "Bu—"

"I know. Badly. I'm sorry."

Weller had some cotton balls and a couple of airtight plastic bags and a little screw-top sample jar that Patel had given him, along with an old pair of tweezers that he could leave behind when he was finished. He'd left some alcohol and clean rags in the space between the two doors so that he could clean up after himself. All he needed now was a sample of McCall's blood, and that wasn't going to be difficult to find. It was everywhere.

He talked as he got ready. Thinking maybe his voice was the last friendly sound McCall would ever hear. "Dr. Patel thinks she might be onto a cure," he said. "That'd be something, don't you think?"

No answer. McCall seemed to have used up whatever energy he had.

"She sends her regards. Nobody else knows I'm here. I believe Liz would kill me."

Something that might have been the root of a ragged smile bent McCall's lips just the slightest.

"I know. As if the virus won't." He sopped up a little blood from the rubber sheet with a cotton ball, and put the ball into the jar. Did it a few times more until the jar was nearly full. "I wish we knew where this thing came from," he said as he screwed the top back on.

McCall drew breath and steadied himself to speak again.

Weller watched him.

Just that one syllable: "Buh—"

"Right," Weller nodded. "Blood."

McCall winced.

"Lots of it." He wiped the jar with a cloth from a rack over the bed. He'd memorized the steps that Patel wanted him to take with the bags and the alcohol, but they would have to wait until he was out in the space between the doors. He looked down one last time at McCall, and said he was sorry that things were going this way for him. He and Bud hadn't bargained for this.

Looking straight into Weller's eyes through the plastic screen of the hazmat helmet, McCall mustered everything he had for one last word. It emerged on breath as faint as a wish, but it was clear and precise and perfect. "Bud." Just that.

And Weller knew.

*

They spent a little time exploring the college. Patel wouldn't mind, or at least that's what Bud said. Janey knew better but she listened to him anyhow, because she wanted to. There were classrooms by the score and academic offices stacked on top of one another and lecture halls shaped like little amphitheaters. There was a complex of overgrown athletic fields that showed where the school's real interests must have lain. That's what Bud said. He said you looked where the money went if you wanted to find out what was important to people, and this was where the money went. There were dormitories that had been ransacked and set afire for some reason. Just blackened shells that still smelled of burning.

Bud said he'd always wished he could have gotten himself an education. Gone to college and made something of himself.

Janey said all he would have wanted from college was to meet some college girls.

He said she was probably right about that. He never got a chance to meet anything in the way of girls. Not when he was younger and not in his line of work now. Not until her.

Janey wasn't having any of that kind of talk. She kidded back as if he'd been kidding. She said they'd both be better off if he'd had a wider range of choices. Maybe he'd go a little easier. Press his case a little less.

Which made Bud think about throttling back some. Taking some other angle if he could figure one out.

*

"Bud," said Weller. "It makes sense, don't you think?"

Patel had to agree. "They didn't weaponize the virus to infect everybody, they weaponized a runner to infect Spartanburg."

"Exactly. They'd never been able to get to Spartanburg before, and it was driving them nuts."

"So they got *us* to help deliver the payload."

Weller stiffened. "We didn't mean to."

Patel looked up from her microscope. "I'm not saying we should feel guilty about it. Just that somebody out there is absolutely coldblooded."

"Not to mention opportunistic."

"And adaptable, too."

"Sounds like the virus," Weller said.

Patel smiled and looked back down. "There are viruses and then there are viruses," she said. "They take many shapes. I've always thought that certain ideas might be the worst contagions in the world, once they take hold."

Word got around fast. It filtered down from Patel with the same certainty that it once filtered down from Oates. The pathways it took were more organic, though. They weren't based on the old military chain of command and they weren't based on the phony town meetings that Oates had instituted to make sure his orders got disseminated. All Patel had to do was mention that Bud was no doubt the one who'd given the virus to his old partner, and word spread through every channel there was. Soon enough the whole town was on the lookout for his return. Some said he'd never show his face in these parts again, and some said otherwise. They said he'd come back with Janey just the way he always did, just as if nothing had happened, purely to take the measure of the ruin he'd caused. After all, what were the chances that McCall could have found out the truth? What were the chances that he could have told anybody even if he had? Bud didn't seem like the type who'd reason all of that stuff out and play it safe, though, the type who'd think things through to every possible conclusion and operate accordingly. He was more the kind who'd come back to gloat over what he'd done.

In other words, he quickly became in their minds a kind of idiotic villain. A dangerous buffoon. A source of merriment and terror in equal parts.

They'd outsmarted him for now, or at least they'd minimized his sting and confined its damage. But you couldn't tell what a person like Bud might be up to next time. So over the next little while Spartanburg closed up again, drawing in upon itself almost as tightly as before. The doors weren't welded shut, but they were most definitely locked. The outdoor fields, tilled and planted so recently, were abandoned once more. Not for fear of something imaginary this time, but for fear of something real.

*

Weller worried like everybody else. He worried about his wife and child, but he also worried about Janey, out there alone in the world with nobody and nothing to protect her from Bud—not to mention whatever trouble Bud might get himself into.

Seven or eight days passed since McCall had first awakened with the virus, two or three of them since Weller had gotten the blood samples. He hadn't seen Patel since he'd dropped them off—she'd been *incommunicado*, not even showing up at mealtimes—but he went to see her now. Asking if she thought there was any chance Bud could have acquired the virus himself during the act of giving it to McCall.

"Sure there is," she said. "Probably a better chance he'll get it than that he won't."

Weller's face fell.

"Since when do you care about Bud?" She said it with the only mischievous smile he'd ever seen her give anyone.

"I'm not thinking about Bud."

"Of course not." Looking back down to a stream of numbers that flew across one of the screens too fast for anyone but an expert to take in.

"He could be spreading it right now."

"Plus we never found the syringe."

"Right."

"I doubt that whoever he was working for provided very much training in the way of sanitary procedures."

"But they wouldn't want the virus getting out."

"They wouldn't have expected him to keep the syringe, either."

"I suppose you're right."

They were both silent for a minute. The numbers streamed past. Patel drew a sudden breath.

"That's it," she said, raising a finger and pointing. "*That's* what we're looking for."

"The cure?"

"It's a start."

*

They found what turned out to have been the faculty club. An open lounge with high windows and big leather chairs torn to bits and lived in at some remote time by vermin. Blackened fireplaces at each end and a couple of tables still standing but the rest surely used for firewood. Faint rectangles on the walls where paintings had been taken down and burned instead of admired. Sooner or later, nobody had had time to admire anything.

Beyond the lounge and down a hallway was a dining room that looked pretty much the same. A few of the tall windows were broken, and the world had come in through the gaps to reclaim its own the way it always does. Grass and low brush and a couple of young trees leaning toward the sun. Janey pictured this place fifty years from now when the trees had grown up and lifted the roof clean away and let in more nature. She wondered how much would be left of this building in the end. Maybe the foundation. Maybe not even that, if you gave it enough time.

They found the kitchen behind the dining room. Ransacked the way you would expect, as if savages had been through and then wild animals and finally a hurricane to lay it all flat. They opened the swinging door to a pantry that was empty but for the bones of something that had died there and then been eaten itself. A raccoon it looked like. They walked into the walk-in cooler not even knowing what it was. A cell perhaps, although why they'd have had a thing like that in such a place was a mystery. If it wasn't a cell then maybe it was a fallout shelter from back in the days when people thought the world would end in fallout. A fast nuclear disaster instead of the slow disaster they'd lived through but just barely. Bud said he'd seen fallout shelters before, and they always had a metal sign with the three yellow triangles inside a black circle. That was how you knew a fallout shelter. There was no a sign on this one, but maybe somebody stole the sign. You couldn't trust people, he said.

There were a couple of cots set up in the cooler, and a couple of sleeping bags heaped on top of them that some creature had used after the people who'd put them there had gone on their way or else just gone off to die. Janey could picture somebody making a last stand there. Behind that metal door and surrounded by more metal, the only opening to the outside world a grate in the floor covering a drain. You could feel pretty safe there, fallout or no fallout. Bud picked up one of the sleeping bags and sniffed it and heaved it into a corner with a curse.

With the sleeping bag gone, Janey pointed toward the cot. Below it, actually, where a steel trunk sat revealed.

Bud fell to his knees. The trunk was unmarked, unscarred, unscathed. Painted green except for the hardware, which looked like nickel and had tarnished a good deal. On the front a padlock held down a hasp that kept it shut. The padlock looked to be in good shape too, although there were some scratch marks around the keyhole from use.

"Somebody took good care of this," he said.

"But they left it behind anyhow."

He pushed at it to test the resistance it gave against the concrete floor. "Too heavy to move," he said. "Although it ain't bolted down." He lifted the padlock a time or two and let it drop. Just letting it clang. Thinking. Pulling on his lip with the other hand. Between the effort of his concentration and the banging of the padlock he didn't even see Janey leave. He only noticed when she came back with a length of metal that would do as a pry bar.

Twenty:

Discoveries

Penny dreamed of something coming near. She was in a very high place—either standing on the roof of the car factory or not standing anywhere at all, just hanging suspended in the middle of the air—and she was looking toward the horizon. People were working in the fields below. She saw them the same way she'd see any ordinary thing in waking life. She saw them with perfect clarity and without especially noticing them. What she did notice was the clarity of her vision, since vision was something that still astonished her. The bright reality of everything.

The people in the fields worked with their hands and with tools and with machinery. They worked methodically and they worked without pausing. The tractors made little distant coughing sounds and the people called to one another in tiny voices and a wind came up from the north and Penny turned into it. Looking in that direction she could see the trail that she and her mother and father had come down a few weeks before, even though she knew that there was no such trail. That they'd just come from out of the woods. Nonetheless, she could see it. She rose up higher. Not on the roof now. She rose up lifted by some urge to take in more and more of her surroundings and although there were clouds all around and she was among them she could still see everything. The people and the tractors and the trail that didn't exist. Other people at work in the building below her feet. Her own suspended self, as if witnessed from a great distance. Wind stroked her hair and tugged at her clothes and she spun in it a little bit like something hanging loose from a rope, but no matter how she spun she always returned to face the same direction. Drawn by the pull of true north.

Something was approaching from that way. Something distant but moving fast. Something whose footsteps didn't so much strike the ground as lift it up from beneath.

If she had been at that moment in a place where words were possible, she might have said that it was something that seemed to have been born from inside the earth itself. Something that had grown under the ground and taken it over and even to some measure become it. Whatever it was, it passed through the world like a shock wave. Forests rose before its passage and fell within its wake, never to rise again. Deep strata of rock rippled. Death lay behind it.

The thing followed the path that she and her parents and the rest of them had come down before, the path that existed only in this dream or vision or whatever else it was, and it gained speed as it came, obliterating every single thing before it. It roared in a voice that was the voice of the world, although Penny was the only person who could hear it. The people below her in the fields worked on, oblivious. The ground beneath their feet trembled in anticipation, but they didn't notice. Eventually they began to stagger and lose their balance, and their machinery began to fail in the presence of the oncoming shock wave, but they never raised their eyes until it was too late.

*

Johnnie Walker Black Label, the bottles said. Blended Scotch Whisky.

Bud ran his finger down the length of one bottle, all the way to the bottom. "Twelve years old," he said with a derisive laugh. "Twelve years old *when?*"

"A long time ago," said Janey.

Bud twisted off the cap and held the mouth of the bottle to his nose and breathed deep. "We are in luck, sweet thing."

"I'm not your sweet thing."

"Have it your way," he said, undeterred. "We're still in luck."

Getting the whole trunkful back to where they were camping required half a dozen trips. Bud made most of them. Janey couldn't see bothering. She could see bothering for water, but not for this. She carried the empty trunk on the first trip but that was all the effort she put in.

To judge by the descending level in the bottle he'd opened, Bud was helping himself to a little of the Johnnie Walker every time he came back to the cooler. She asked him about it and he confessed. As reward, of course, and also as lubrication to make the trips go easier. To remind himself of the point of the whole exercise. You couldn't blame a feller for that, could you?

She said maybe she could and maybe she couldn't. The whisky didn't seem to be speeding him along any. Once while he was gone she took a sip and it tasted like dirt and moss and gasoline all mixed up together.

"The taste" he said when she told him, "ain't the whole reason you drink it." He was sweating. The day wasn't that warm and he was accustomed to traveling great distances under heavy burdens, and here he stood with sweat running down his forehead. He wiped it stinging from his eyes with the brush of a hard knuckle, looking a little disoriented.

He was a long while coming back with the last load. The bottles all had screw tops, and Janey noticed from the seals on them that the bunch he had in his pack had all been opened. No doubt he'd sipped a little bit out of each one on the sly, thinking she would't notice. He deposited them in the trunk and mixed the lot of them together like a man playing a card trick, and then he went over to the table and sat down and addressed himself to the one he'd been working on. Yawning and drooping a little. Saying, "I drank some home brew once, but it wasn't nothing like this." Sloshing some into the bottom of a glass and offering it up to Janey but not even waiting for her refusal before throwing back his head and downing it himself.

*

Refinements would have to wait. There was no telling how much of the drug would cure McCall and how much of it would kill him. He'd die without it, though. That much was plain. Patel herself went in this time, cracking the seals on the paired doors when none of the medics were around. Nowhere near the top of an even-numbered hour. They'd have let her in, if she'd asked. Anybody would have done anything for Dr. Patel. But she didn't want to signal what she was up to or how close she might have gotten. She didn't want to get anybody's hopes up. So she sneaked in the same way Weller had sneaked in before, and she found something that passed for a vein in McCall's forearm, and she shot him full of the compound she'd been working on.

The drug had worked fast in the lab, but there was no telling how it would perform inside the collapsing system of a dying man. If it worked at all.

*

The whisky took hold of Bud in a hurry. It made him weak and sleepy and confused. It made him forget where his hands and feet were. It made him slur his words and bump into walls. Now that darkness had come on, it was worse. They had some candles from the faculty club burning here and there, but he still kept dodging shadows and running into walls every time he tried going anywhere.

Maybe the stuff had gone bad over the years. He had the presence of mind to maintain that thought for exactly one second before his brain skittered off somewhere else. Before he took another drink.

He got talking. Not clearly, but insistently. He'd been a talker all along, but under the influence of all of that whisky the talk just wouldn't stop coming. His mind darted like a waterbug and the words swam after it as best they could. They never quite caught up, though, and they never followed in anything like a straight line, and it frustrated him.

He talked about how big the world was, and how the only thing he wanted was to show it all to Janey. Everything he'd seen and then some. Things he hadn't even seen yet and didn't know anything about.

He confessed that when they'd found the whisky he'd hoped to get her a little drunk on it with the idea that maybe something would happen between the two of them. He told her he was sorry for that.

He told her he needed a new partner now that McCall was dead. He told her he was sorry for that, too.

"Dead to *you*, I guess." She wondered what might have come between them.

"No no no no," he said, shaking his head from side to side. "Not just dead to me. Dead to everybody. *Dead* dead."

"He was fine the last time I saw him."

The head-shaking had disrupted his equilibrium and he answered slowly, one word at a time, collecting himself little by little. "You weren't the last to see him. McCall, I mean. To see McCall." A second blinked past. "I seen him last."

No answer from Janey. Just a look that said why didn't Bud go someplace and lie down until he felt more like himself.

But he wasn't interested in sleeping it off. Not yet. He sat in the dim candlelight and looked from the whisky to Janey's pale face and back to the whisky as if he were trying to figure out something. Some other way of explaining himself. "McCall's dead," he finally said.

"So you said."

"Did I mention that?"

"You did."

He smiled and reached for the bottle. Part of him was satisfied that he'd communicated at least the basics. "It wasn't my idea," he said, sloshing some into his glass.

"What idea was that?"

He breathed deep. "Giving him the bug. Shooting him up with it. I never done nothing like that before." He tilted the glass and got some whisky and his tongue and let it sit there. After a minute he pursed his lips and swallowed. "I done some bad things, all right. Don't get me wrong. I stole stuff that weren't mine. I lied and took advantage." Wandering off down a road of reminiscence.

She drew him back. "What bug are you talking about?"

"The big one. The one that killed everything. The virus."

"It died out. It's gone."

"There was some left." He looked sleepier than ever. "There's still some of everything, if you look." He raised the glass as evidence.

"And you found it."

He yawned and set the glass down on the floor. He sat for a minute and started to say something, but then he began to collapse toward sleep, sliding forward a little on his legs and backward on his elbows at the same time. Flattening out.

She stood and walked over and pushed at him with the toe of her boot. "Hold on," she said. "You're telling me you went looking for the virus and then you used it to kill McCall."

"No. Yes." Rolling over on his side, toward the wall.

"It doesn't make any sense, Bud."

"I wanted to make room for you," he said.

"That's bullshit."

"All right."

"If you'd wanted McCall dead, there were easier ways."

"All right."

"With the two of you out there alone in the wilderness."

"Sure."

"Plus you'd have had to bring the virus with you. You'd have had to have it in your pack when you met me."

"I guess you're right."

"Why would you be walking around with a thing like that?"

"I don't know. Search me."

The harder she thought about it the dumber the idea seemed, and the more questions she asked the stupider Bud got, until there was no figuring out what had happened if anything. There was no talking to him at all. So she took a candle and found another room and pushed some furniture against the door to keep it closed in case he got any ideas, and then she tried to get some sleep.

*

When she shouldered the furniture away and came out again in the morning, the place stank of whisky and vomit. Bud himself was still curled up against the wall, but it was clear that he'd been up during the night. Not just emptying his stomach, either. He'd been ransacking his own belongings, going through them like the lowest and most desperate of thieves, looking for God knew what.

She wasn't in any hurry to rouse him and he didn't awaken on his own despite her moving around. She opened windows and got out some breakfast. Not making much noise but not particularly trying to keep it down either. She ate sitting at a table grimed with lost years. History was set down on it in layers. Dust and then more dust with the tracks of mice in it and then more dust obliterating the tracks once the mice had died out. She ate marveling at how the dust kept coming regardless. The pressure of the air itself against the high ceilings must have some erosive power. She wondered how long it would take for the air alone to reduce the building where she sat to nothing but microscopic powder. Not as long as a person might think, she decided. Decay worked on its own schedule. It didn't honor yours.

A breeze blew in through the windows and the air in the room got better and Bud still lay snoring against the wall. She finished eating and began to gather up the things they'd collected for the trip back to Spartanburg. There wasn't much, unless you counted the whisky, which she didn't. Half of what they had she could fit into her backpack without even trying. The other half would go into Bud's if she could keep him from loading up on bottles of that Johnnie Walker. If she could bear traveling with him after last night.

Maybe she could compact his gear while he was still sawing wood. Get rid of a few things he'd never miss. She bent over his pack, thinking that if he woke up and caught her she would just say that she was cleaning up the mess he'd made in the night. At one point she lifted it up to check its weight, and that was when she found the syringe. The thing he'd been looking for in the night. He'd found it and then in some burst of alcoholic logic he'd hidden it under the pack, and now here it was, come to light. A small thing with a needle not much bigger than a hair jutting from one end, the inside of its glass body coated with some greasy yellow substance that looked like poison and certainly was. The thing was wrapped loosely in rags and she was glad she hadn't touched them. She regretted she'd even touched the pack. Who knew how that stuff traveled from surface to surface? Who knew how much or how little she'd need to be infected herself?

Who knew whether it had to be injected or just touched in order to do its work? Who knew how many times she'd been exposed to it over the days of this last trip?

She dropped the pack and went over to wake him up. Thinking she'd disliked him before but by God she hated him now. The bastard lying there snoring in his own mess. The mess of his vomit and this other bigger mess. And then, as she drew back to jam her boot into his rib cage as hard as she could, she realized that by shooting up his partner with the virus, Bud had doomed every single person she'd ever known in this whole world. Everybody she cared about. And so she hated him more. She hated him about as much as one person could hate another one.

She knew she couldn't go home again, though. And she knew she'd need his help to get anywhere else.

Twenty-One:

Past and Future

The kid's name was Jim. He'd been born like every other kid he knew, born into the saddle—in his case a well-greased and deeply weathered thing that his father had made. The kid had always clung to that saddle. The father, on the other hand, he'd lost back when he was too young to notice. It could have been any of a thousand things that got him. A flooded river or a feral pig or some ravenous creature whose ancestors had once upon a time been bears. An altercation with some other grown man at cross purposes. People didn't talk about him much, and when they did they mainly sighed and said they hoped Jim didn't grow up the same way his old man had grown up. *Trouble,* they said. Looking for trouble and doomed to it. They said if the kid's mother hadn't died in childbirth things might have been different. The old man might have had something to occupy him. Something to stop him from making an enemy of the whole world and every last thing in it.

The kid tossed Hutchinson his pack and shouldered one of his own. Led him out the rear of the barn and along a footpath toward the paddock. He moved silently under dim starlight and high cloud, and Hutchinson did the same, leaning down to the kid's level when he had the opportunity and keeping his voice low. "I don't think we ought to be disturbing the horses," he said.

"We ain't disturbing them," the kid said. "We're stealing a couple."

Hutchinson scanned the fenceline. "There's bound to be somebody keeping watch."

The kid turned toward Hutchinson and gave him a smile visible even in the near dark. "You're looking at him," he said.

They stopped at a tack shed. The shelves and hooks and wooden pegs on the walls were all mounted low, and Hutchinson could see that this was where the children stored their equipment. He didn't know anything about horses or keeping horses or riding them for that matter, and in a low voice he asked if any of this gear would fit him. The kid snickered and reassured him that the main thing was whether or not it fit the horse. The horse was the one with the crucial vote in the matter.

*

Penny told her mother about the vision or whatever it was in which she'd found herself suspended high in the air, witnessing the approach of some great and malevolent and transformative thing.

"You're thinking of the virus," Liz said. "It's perfectly understandable that you would."

The two of them were sitting near the swings by the indoor ballfield that her father had traversed so long ago in his pursuit of the car that set all of this in motion. The ballfield where children played once more, now that the outside world was closed off again.

"I don't think so," said Penny. "That bad man brought the virus a while ago, right? He had it with him when we all came, didn't he?"

"I suppose so. That's what everybody thinks."

"So if I was going to have a dream about it, I'd have dreamed about it then." She stood up and took a seat in one of the swings and began to drift forward and back. "I never dream about the past," she said, certain as time. "I only dream about the future."

"Don't be silly."

But she wasn't being silly, and in her heart Liz knew it.

"I'm not. I'm just thinking."

Liz watched her.

"If it *is* the virus I dreamed about, then it's coming back."

*

They walked the horses out of the paddock and through the southern gate and out into the foothills, clicking their tongues softly and offering up crabapples and cakes of grain. They had been careful to close the gate behind them, but they hadn't dared risk the time or commotion of saddling up. The kid had just tossed a rope over each of the horses and that was that. Nothing more was necessary. The horses knew him well and came along as companionably as dogs.

They walked that way for a couple of hours, the boy ahead on a trail that he and the horses knew by heart. As time went by Hutchinson decided he could have done this blindfolded, as long as he'd kept his shoulder to the horse's side. The horse was gentle and confident and he was growing comfortable with her. He still felt that way when they moved into a copse of trees and tethered the horses and lay down to catch some sleep before dawn. His thinking changed, though, and all of his false confidence corrected itself, when morning arrived. When the time came to cinch up and climb into the saddle for some serious travel.

The kid had never seen a person who didn't know how to handle a horse, but he was seeing one now. He didn't think it was funny, even though any other child of his background and upbringing might have. Any other child might have found Hutchinson's ignorance hilarious at best and pathetic at worst. But Jim wasn't any other child and he wasn't built that way. He'd been looking up to Hutchinson until now, and he wasn't about to begin laughing at him—or, worse, *doubting* him—over one failure that couldn't be helped. They had thrown their lots in together. They were a team. And if part of the bargain was that the kid had to teach the man something from time to time, then so be it.

His attitude surprised Hutchinson. Hutchinson had seen it all in Black Rose. He'd seen every kind of cruelty and derision known to mankind, the varieties of institutional and personal humbling that could break a man down so far and so completely that he'd be robbed of the will to restore himself. Abuse of that kind was a necessary part of the military, because unless you'd done everything possible to demolish a man and failed, you didn't know when he'd collapse on his own. You couldn't risk that, so it didn't matter if you ruined a few perfectly decent men and left them weeping in the dust. Individual losses were the price of building something more important.

And now here was this kid—and kids were typically the cruelest of beasts, weren't they?—here was this kid who looked upon an older man's shortcomings not with mockery and contempt but with sympathy and compassion. This big-hearted kid who looked up to him while not minding if he had a fault or two. Jim walked him patiently through the basics, and got both him and the horse calmed down and working together, and maintained an encouragingly slow pace as they began to make their way upward into the mountains.

Hutchinson followed along behind, trying to do every single thing exactly as the kid did it, and he asked himself what kind of ruin he'd have made of this poor orphan child in a different world.

*

Dr. Patel didn't figure that Janey would come back. She didn't think she'd be able to. Not out there with Bud, full of himself as he must be over his cowardly work of hired murder. First he wouldn't want to part company with her, and second he wouldn't want her to come back and get eaten by the virus. So he'd talk her into something. You could be sure of that. Bud was a talker. He thought talking could get him into or out of anything.

Plus it had become clear that he was willing to do more than just talk. God only knew what he might be willing to try.

She hadn't checked on McCall since she'd given him the needle, not knowing whether a second dose would make any difference and having barely enough of the drug for a second dose and possessing no raw materials to make more. She trusted that the medics would speak up if he began to show signs of improvement. But she'd injected him a day and a half ago, and it was high time she looked for herself.

If he showed no signs that the drug was working, then she'd have failed. Tragic as that outcome would be, it would also clarify things. They'd have to resign themselves to living here in the car factory under lockdown, hoping that the virus never came back. If the drug was taking hold, on the other hand, things would get more complicated. Lacking supplies to synthesize more of it, their only hope would be to share the formula with the world—but the world seemed awfully far away.

*

The kids were playing kickball. Out for recess like any other children, although here in the car factory the word *out* didn't mean exactly what it meant anywhere else. It meant *in*. Still, they weren't studying. Just running around, hollering at each other, blowing off steam.

Penny was in the outfield. The ball rarely got that far, and when it did she would glance up too late to calculate its path. She was a mystery to the other children, and not entirely because she hadn't grown up them. She was perfectly capable with the ball, fast on her feet and sharp-eyed and just about tireless, but she couldn't seem to keep her mind on the game. She hated to let her teammates down by missing a catch, though. And because they could see that on her face, they never gave her much trouble. They just posted her in the deep outfield, out by the empty loading docks where the ball almost never went and she could do the least harm.

She was dreaming again today. Looking off down the lane that led to the commercial district and the residential district and home. People came and went down there. She always thought that if she looked hard enough she might spot her mother among them, even though she knew that Liz was off working someplace else. Everybody had a job here in the car factory. When they'd lived in the Northeastern Empowerment Zone, her mother had stayed home and kept the house going while her father did repair work and cobbled together things he could sell. She wasn't entirely certain how all of that operated, but she knew what the result was. Here, everybody had a job and everybody had exactly what they needed in the way of food and so forth, but looking back at the old days she wasn't sure that it was an improvement.

So she was dreaming again. Remembering days past and picturing days to come. Aware of the other children running and shouting. Conscious of the vague movements of vague figures at the end of the lane. And when the ball came sailing her way and the small figure of Dr. Patel appeared around a bright and distant corner, the synchrony caused something in her brain to go haywire.

"He's getting better!" she shouted to nobody, to everybody, to the vanishing and impossibly remote figure of Dr. Patel. "He's going to be fine!" And then she collapsed to the ground.

Twenty-Two:

Awakenings

Bud woke up from a dream of bewilderment and blood. In the world of the dream, as in the waking world itself, everything had gone wrong. His way forward was unclear. His footsteps were upward bound and painfully slow if he could take them at all. Someone was bleeding and it might have been him and it might not. Who it was varied moment by moment, in the way of dreams. Nothing held fast except struggle and uncertainty.

The toe of Janey's boot in a tender spot below his rib cage awakened him to an entirely different class of misery, one more complicated and nuanced than the vague dream he'd awakened from, but doubly harsh on account of its variety and specificity. A mouth that tasted like something had died about halfway down his throat. A head that felt like a bomb had gone off inside it. A former partner that he'd shot up with certain doom. And a woman that he'd had his heart set on, suddenly turned against him.

Not without reason, either. He had it coming. No question about that. So once his head cleared and his ears quit ringing and his consciousness began to coalesce, he was surprised to hear the words she was saying.

"Let's get out of here."

*

Hutchinson consulted his Black Rose compass now and then, but compass or no compass the directional choices were limited. In the mountains, and especially on horseback, you couldn't just go straight in any direction even if you wanted to. You went pretty much where the topography decided you'd go, and if you had other ideas you worked them out little by little over the long term. In general, though, he and the kid seemed to be headed south. The kid said that his people mainly went east when they went anywhere, into the foothills and down into the lowlands by the coast. The landscape was wide open down there. The mountains were good for secrecy, he said, but his people never required much by way of secrecy. The horses gave them mobility and speed, which were better than secrecy any day of the week.

Hutchinson could see by how lonesome and trackless the mountains were that the kid was telling him the truth. There were animal prints up here, but not hoofprints. Game trails, but not horse trails. No sign of man whatsoever. Which didn't mean people didn't come here, but did suggest that they didn't come often.

The weather as they traveled was fine and the air was clear and high clouds raced miles overhead, reminding Hutchinson that he and the kid were just the tiniest of creatures on a small rock surrounded by an ocean of air. They lived on greens and fruit and small game. Pods that yielded up fleshy seeds, and ripe red berries that were everywhere in the alpine meadows now that summer had begun to wane. They netted flashing trout in high mountain streams.

Hutchinson learned trust, hearing the kid say that the rabbits and squirrels around here were good eating no matter what anyone else told him and taking it for gospel. The only gospel he had. He learned patience, keeping his eyes open and devising all manner of snares and traps and waiting out his prey on whatever schedule it might keep.

Sometimes he wished he still had his pistol and sometimes he didn't miss it at all. That teacher must have dealt with it. He thought about it less and less as the days went by. It was something from a different world, a different life.

The kid, for his part, learned resourcefulness and self-reliance. Back home his people had divided up labor the way that any civilized group will, but two wanderers in a mountain wilderness couldn't divide anything but such spoils as might come to hand. If there was work, you did it. And there was always work. He played around a little when he could and he made mistakes the way any child will. He thought maybe he could make a hunting bow, but although it looked nice and he'd tempered it over a low fire with squirrel grease it wouldn't shoot straight no matter how he tried. Maybe it was his arrows and maybe not, maybe it was him, but for every minute he spent fussing with archery equipment Hutchinson spent a minute idly minding his traps, and in the end it was Hutchinson who kept them fed.

They pressed on. And the rabbits didn't kill them and the berries didn't kill them and the world seemed more or less trustworthy and constant, if not exactly kind.

*

"New York is what I'm thinking," said Bud. "We sure as hell ain't going back to Spartanburg."

"New York. What would you do in New York?"

"Pick up the keys to the city, for starters." Sitting there on the linoleum floor with his back pressed against the wall. Not looking like anybody's idea of a hero. "Enjoy my ticker tape parade."

"What's that? What's a ticker tape parade?"

"It's something they used to have. They'd throw one when you did something big and they wanted to show you how great they thought you were."

"So you think they're going to throw you a parade."

"Sure. I'm a big deal up in New York."

"I don't think so."

"Maybe not yet. But I will be when I file my report."

"Saying you killed your partner."

Bud tried to stand up, but he slid back down the wall. His head weighed nothing and it weighed a ton. "Screw my partner," he said.

Janey shook her head. "So you stand by what you did."

"They wanted Spartanburg wiped off the map, and they give me the weapon, and I delivered it."

"Who? Who wanted Spartanburg gone?"

"Now it's time I got the rest of my reward."

"Who were you working for?"

"Maybe I'll stop in Washington and get myself named a five-star general."

"Black Rose, then?"

"Black Rose give me the job. The pay was AmeriBank scrip. You tell me."

"Never mind where the scrip came from. You did it for pay, and you still think you deserve a parade."

"You don't know until you ask."

She picked up her pack and adjusted it on her shoulders. Looking around to see if she'd forgotten anything. "If we can't go back to Spartanburg," she said at last, "New York will have to do."

*

McCall was back on his feet in a couple of days. Eating like a horse. Circling the perimeter of the examining room and buzzing with reawakened energy and interrogating the medics nonstop as to how he'd ended up here and how long he'd been out of commission. He was still bandaged all over and he was still bleeding in places and he still had a thousand bruises that dripped purple and gray and yellow behind almost every inch of his skin, but otherwise his recovery was astonishing even to Dr. Patel, who'd engineered it.

She asked him how he felt, and his answer was simple.

"I'm pissed the hell off," he said.

She asked him to lie down, please, and when he found out that it wasn't for an examination—she just wanted him to get his heart rate under control—he sat up again and sprang from the table and circled once more.

"Please," she said. "Mr. McCall."

"Damn him," he said. "Damn him to hell."

"Bud?"

McCall nodded with a slow fury.

"Bud's gone, Mr. McCall. And we're still here. I'd call that a victory."

It seemed to McCall that she was just trying to placate him, and he kept circling.

"We *won*, Mr. McCall. That's something."

McCall stopped to correct her. *"You* won," he said.

"All right." Waiting for what would come next, if anything.

McCall raised a trembling finger. "I brought him here. I trusted him. I told him not to take that deal and he took it anyhow, took it without my knowing, and then he turned on me."

"The deal," she said. "Tell me about it."

"Drop a bomb on Spartanburg," he said. "Poison the well. You can figure it out."

"Oh, I already have. There's been plenty of time to think about it while you've been on that table. I just wanted to make sure."

"How long was I down, anyway?"

"You're still down."

"Really, how long?"

"Ten days, maybe."

McCall shook his head. "That's a long time."

She raised a hand and pointed at him. "That's why you're in such poor shape."

"I ought to be dead, though."

"True."

"Has anybody ever recovered from the virus?"

"Not that I know of."

"So I'm a miracle."

She shrugged.

McCall corrected himself. "I'm *your* miracle."

Dr. Patel smiled.

*

Saddling up for the day's ride, he swung the kid's pack up from the ground and thought it felt heavy. The kid was off taking a leak, so he looked inside and discovered his Black Rose pistol. Once he'd seen it he left it right where it was. Put the pack back down where he'd found it. If the kid had thought he'd need it to protect himself against him, he'd learned differently by now. But there might still be uses for it.

The kid taught him about looking after horses. They got to be a unit, the two of them and the two animals. Working together and relying on one another and trusting each other equally. Hutchinson recalled what he'd learned about military history, back to the War Between the States and farther back than that. Back to the War of 1812 and the Revolution. Not just in America, either, but elsewhere. All over Europe and Asia.

He pictured the cavalries of old. Hundreds of men with hundreds of horses. He thought they must have felt unstoppable.

Twenty-Three:

Outbreak

If Janey was ever going to see New York, now was the time. She'd been close before. Close enough that technically at least you could say she'd seen it already. From the deck of the George Washington Bridge, out over the Hudson River, looking south toward the high towers and green overgrowth and low ruins of Manhattan. But she hadn't been concentrating on New York at that moment. She'd been looking for Black Rose helicopters, and trying to figure out how to jack remotely into their control systems.

It seemed so long ago. It seemed like years. But what had it been, really? How long since she and Weller and his wife and kid had been high-tailing it north in that big maroon BMW, evading Black Rose and looking for Dr. Patel's outpost and angling for some entry point into the fenced-off Empowerment Zone? Six weeks? Maybe not even that.

Yet here she was, presented with a second chance to see the big city. The cosmopolitan home not just of Management but of Owner-ship—Ownership in spades, thanks to the concentration there not just of AmeriBank headquarters but outposts of pretty much every major corpora-tion that was left. National Motors. PharmAgra. Mutual Electric. Real-News.

Seeing the city meant seeing how the other half lived, even though the other half didn't add up to anything like half. Maybe they were one or two percent. The one or two percent that had everything, while people like Janey had nothing. Less than nothing, now that Bud had gone and

139

dropped a bomb in the middle of Spartanburg. But where else was she supposed to go? And how else was she supposed to get there?

He knew the way. If he didn't, he acted as if he did. He had a compass in his head and between that and the sun and the stars they tracked northeast day by day, no problem. Eating what they'd brought, keeping their profiles low, until before long they were in familiar territory—familiar to Janey from her trip north with Weller, familiar to Bud from everything he'd learned in a lifetime of running. There were villages here that Janey wouldn't have discovered in a million years, and he knew where every one of them was. Scientific outposts and dangerous revolutionary hotbeds and blockaded survivalist freak shows, each with its own history and customs and relationship to the world at large. Everybody in them knew Bud. They all owed him something or planned on owing him something one day. He and Janey started eating a little better, and drinking water that they could more or less trust.

If it occurred to anyone that Bud might have something in his backpack capable of killing them all—capable in fact of killing just about everybody left everywhere—they didn't show any sign of it. The idea was probably old news to most of them, in particular to the hard-core survivalists. Everybody was a survivalist these days, but those who'd specialized in it all along couldn't see that. They'd defined themselves that way for generations, and the case was closed. They'd inherited the mantle from their fathers and from their father's fathers before them, old-timers long dead who'd spent their lives digging underground bunkers and stockpiling food and building up extravagant caches of weaponry. Strategizing about a future that they figured would fall one day like a curtain, like a boot, like a bomb, when the truth was that the real thing had arrived so slowly that their descendants were still waiting for it. Still holding out for the worst.

*

There was an end to the mountains, of course. There was an end to everything. They came to a narrow precipice with no way to go but back or down, and Hutchinson asked the kid what he thought, and the kid sat tight-lipped. Only the horses answered, shying and whickering and turning tentative. Spooked.

"We can't stay up here forever," Hutchinson said after a while. "And besides, I thought you wanted to see the world."

"I don't know what I wanted to see. I'd seen enough of home, was all."

"Welcome to the club. Be glad that that kind of thinking didn't land you in Black Rose the way it landed me." Taking up the reins and pulling the horse's head to one side a little more roughly than he'd once thought would be required. The horse a living being with its own needs and opinions, resisting but finally making up its mind that maybe Hutchinson was right. Or if not right then at least in charge.

"I can't speak for the food down there," the kid said, pitching his voice above the scuffle and scrape of the horses' hooves. "There's lots of acreage that would have been cultivated once upon a time. You don't know what went into the dirt and you don't know what'll come out of it."

"Who raised you to be so cautious?"

"I ain't cautious."

"I didn't say there was anything wrong with being cautious."

The kid sniffed. Hutchinson had him there.

"In my experience, son, the man who isn't careful is generally the first man to get killed."

"But you want to go down anyhow."

"I do," said Hutchinson. "But cautiously."

*

The greenhouse complex pretty much ran on water. Everything was hydroponic. There'd been a time when hydroponics was the stuff of science fiction, but now it was just temperamental old technology that was breaking down all the time and needed more maintenance work than anyone had time for. And yet they persisted, because for the duration of the foreseeable and unforeseeable future, hydroponic vegetables were going to be the only kind of vegetables they'd have.

If you'd asked the men who built this glassed-in facility in the first place—thirty or forty years before the Great Dying, back when the disaster looming over the whole world was a nuclear bomb or a terrorist strike or some kind of electromagnetic pulse that would shut down everything that ran on electricity—if you'd asked them how long these hydroponics were supposed to keep on functioning they'd have said a couple of years. Just until civilization sorted itself out again and the lunatics either gave up or ran off and the air cleared itself the way it will. A couple of years, tops. Until Mother Nature came to her senses.

The problem was that nobody expected Mother Nature to get poisoned and not care. To get poisoned almost beyond recovery and then to stay poisoned. That was the thing about nature. It swallowed up everything, it *became* everything. It tolerated and even fostered things that might not be good for it and certainly weren't good for you. GMO's, for instance. Genetically Modified Organisms. What organism wasn't genetically modified, when you got down to it? According to the scientists every single organism on earth was the result of modification, ever since the very first one blinked a couple of times down there at the bottom of some ocean and sprouted a couple of legs and decided to crawl out and see the world.

Sometimes a modification that popped up didn't work so well, and when that happened the poor altered creature didn't have a chance. If it was a fish and it sprouted legs, it got a one-way ticket to the beach. If it sprouted wings, though, it was a dead end and nobody even mourned its loss.

That all changed once scientists began to modify living stuff for their own purposes. The scientists wouldn't take *no* for an answer. If they wanted to put something into a green bean that would kill any rabbit that dared take a bite of it, they went right ahead and doctored the plant and killed the rabbit. And here's the problem: the next thing you knew, Mother Nature had adopted that modified plant and made it her own. Incorporated its genetic makeup into the next generation of green beans and the one after that and the one after that.

Woe unto rabbits the world over.

And woe unto human beings, too. Unless some other random event stepped in to help out. Unless, as in this case, somebody a few generations prior had thought—for reasons of his own—to assemble out of glass and rubber and plastic a sealed environment for growing crops in purified water.

In that case, you had a future.

*

The whole place smelled like mold and rotting rubber and heat, but the tomatoes were damned good. That was the promise Bud had made, and for once he knew exactly what he was talking about. The tomatoes were damned good, as were the peppers and the squash and the asparagus and everything else. Right down to the Brussels sprouts, which were the last of their kind in the whole hemisphere and nobody knew it. Nobody anywhere else missed them. Nobody else even knew they'd ever existed, except for a certain transplanted Frenchman who cooked for Ownership in New York—for Anderson Carmichael, in fact—and the Frenchman was keeping his mouth shut.

These, though, were marvels. Perfectly elegant miniature cabbages, little unfolding astonishments of green, green, green.

"You're sure they wouldn't have grown bigger if you'd left them alone?" Janey asked, reluctant to let anything, even potential, go to waste.

The tall man across the table very nearly laughed, but he caught himself at the last instant. "No, ma'am," he said. He was dignified, reserved in his manner, almost courtly. The same went for everyone here in this little secret outpost, where the oldest and simplest of foodstuffs still grew and the oldest and simplest of courtesies still reigned. "That's as big as they'll get."

"Why haven't I known about these before?"

The man across the table lifted his eyebrows.

Bud shrugged.

The old man across the table tilted his head about five degrees to one side and looked questioningly at Bud. "I'd assumed—"

Bud shrugged again. "Look," he said, "if somebody wanted Brussels sprouts, I'd'a known right where to come." He gave a smile as big as the emptiness behind it, "I ain't your salesman," he said. As if that explained all there was to know about their relationship.

The man across the table didn't look happy, but he also didn't look as if he wanted to advertise that fact with company around. "Very well," he said. "Just keep your ears open. And if one of your usual customers happens to mention such a need, we'll be happy to oblige."

They were sitting on a verandah behind the main house. The hydroponics operation was half below-ground and half above, a network of chained greenhouses whose glass had largely mossed over both inside and out. Only as much light got in as was absolutely required, and the buildings blended in with the green hills around them. All the better for secrecy in a world where secrecy was crucial. Going unnoticed was as important to this group's endurance as the crops they raised.

They kept to themselves, but that didn't mean they were ignorant of the outside world. *Worlds* might have been a better way to put it, since there were so many of them. Little separate realities here and there in the wilderness beyond the margins of the Empowerment Zones, linked only by runners like Bud if they were linked at all. They kept to themselves, and now they all sat on the verandah in the shade of a big vine-covered house that looked as if it had been ruined and left to rot during the War Between the States, no more than two dozen individuals, men and women and children alike, soldiering on toward their own isolated end.

"I got nothing for you this time," Bud said, wiping his mouth on the back of his hand. "Things have been a little rough lately."

No one asked what he might mean by that.

"Tell you the truth," he said, "I'm kind of getting things started all over. It's a little bit of a blank slate right now." He showed his empty hands.

The old man across the table nodded. "That's fine. You know you're always welcome at our table."

"I know it," said Bud.

"Whether you have something to trade or not."

"I know. I appreciate it. I appreciate your hospitality."

"And that goes for your friend McCall, too," said the man.

Silence. Bud didn't look at Janey and Janey didn't look at Bud.

The man across the table watched them not looking at each other, and took note of it. "I don't know that I've ever seen one of you without the other." He turned to the woman seated alongside him. "Mother," he said, "do you recall ever seeing Bud without McCall, or vice versa?"

"I don't believe I do, Father."

A handful of children began moving among the tables, clearing away plates and refilling water glasses.

"Did you boys have a falling out?"

"You could say that."

The old patriarch nodded slowly. "That would explain having to start up your business all over again, I suppose."

"Yes, sir. It sure would."

The man took a long drink of water, and then he placed the empty glass down on the table. "It sounds as if you got the dirty end of the stick, as they say."

"Could be."

"I'm sorry to hear that, Bud."

"Likewise."

"Why would a thing like that happen to a person like you?"

"I don't know." Staring at the empty glass. "Just lucky, I guess."

*

The next time she came by the infirmary to check on McCall, he was gone. Nobody had seen him leave. It looked as if he'd helped himself to a clean set of overalls from the medics' closet and maybe a first aid kit, but other than that he'd just vanished. Patel didn't waste time with the medics and she didn't bother going to Oates. Where she went was the machine shop, to see Weller.

When she came through the door he shut down his torch and lifted the battered visor of his welding helmet. She told him that McCall was gone, and he frowned and scratched behind an ear and said, "I guess we weren't the only ones who figured you could do as you like while the medics were busy someplace else."

"I guess not."

"Look on the bright side, though. You should be proud of yourself. You got him back on his feet."

She looked a little startled.

"Take your victories where you can find them, Doc."

She smiled a little tentative smile, but it died fast. Her face grew serious again. "We don't know how he'll do, Henry. He might relapse. He might still be contagious."

Weller nodded. "So where'd he get off to?"

"Wherever he thinks Bud went, would be my guess."

*

Sunrise, and Hutchinson and the kid sat exposed on a ridgeline watching the eastern sky bloom. Feeling like a pair of gods or something. The only ones in the whole world to witness this except the horses. There was a good bit of light up where they sat, but there wasn't much down below. The valleys to the east were still in darkness, and to the north and south the only points of light were early glimmers on the highest peaks.

They sat together and watched the daily rebirth of the world until all at once the kid thrust out an arm toward some brief glint in the valley below. Putting out his hand as if to catch it the way he'd have caught a firefly in an earlier time. "You see that?"

Hutchinson saw it. It glimmered a little, perhaps because of its remoteness, but by and large it held steady for a minute or so before vanishing just as suddenly as it had appeared. Leaving the valley darker for its absence.

"Glass," Hutchinson said.

The kid shrugged. It was a word he'd heard but not a thing he'd seen.

"It's glass, I think. A window maybe. There's some kind of building down there."

They sat quietly for a minute, squinting into the red darkness, searching for the thing they'd seen before but couldn't see now. That little glint.

Then there it was again. That same wavering light that lasted no more than a few seconds and only if you held your head at just the right angle. A gleam as solitary and ineffable as a falling star.

"It was a little lower that time," said the kid.

"You think?"

"Maybe. It seemed that way to me. Like it moved."

The pair of them sitting absolutely still, intent as hunters. Blending into the world and waiting for a sign of some other thing in motion.

"There," said Hutchinson.

The kid didn't see it right away but he angled his head a notch and saw it now. Just lifting his chin to raise his eyes by an inch or so. That little made the difference, and now he sat entranced for the seconds it took for this third appearance of whatever it was to glimmer and glimmer again and then vanish.

"Damn."

"You were right," said Hutchinson. "It was even lower that time."

"It's moving," said the kid.

"I don't think so," said Hutchinson. "I think what we've seen is actually three different things. Three different instances."

The sun fully broke the horizon, and light streamed everywhere.

"I don't think we'll be seeing any more, though. Not now."

They waited, and soon enough the day proved Hutchinson correct. There was only light in the valley below. Pools and lakes of it. Finally an ocean. By and by the kid pulled his attention away and hopped up and went to see about the horses. Hutchinson followed, his legs a little weary and one of his knees hurting. Not old, but definitely feeling his age compared to the youth of the kid. Realizing the obligation that one generation has to the next. To pass down what little it knows.

*

McCall went excruciatingly slowly, but he almost never stopped moving. That was the key. If he couldn't catch Bud by speed or stealth, he'd catch him by sheer perseverance. Conserve his energy. Release it to himself in the smallest of doses. Sleep as little as possible, creeping through the woods and the fields and the byways as slowly by day as by night.

There was a trancelike quality to his movement, a kind of deep and willful self-hypnosis, his disorientation augmented by the blood he'd lost and the high fever he'd only recently undergone. He seemed barely contained by his own body, and he wouldn't have been surprised if at any moment he should prove himself—by accomplishing some miracle, like taking flight or hearing the voices of people far away—to be dead.

But he wasn't dead, and he wasn't dying. At least not immediately. He was pressing on.

*

That night they made a fire on a rocky outcropping. It was a way of cooking their supper and a way of advertising themselves to anyone down below who might care to know about their presence. Eventually it became a way of staying warm as the night wore on. The two of them with their backs against a rock wall that had been warmed a little by the fire but certain to go cold again soon enough. You couldn't get rock warm enough deep enough to last the night. Yet you got whatever kind of a head start you could manage against the cold.

They sat looking out over the fire into the starlit darkness. Listening to the horses moving among some low trees a little distance away. "So," the kid asked. "What were they? Those things we saw this morning?"

"Windows," said Hutchinson. "Windows in a three-story house. Simple as that." Scratching a rectangle onto the rock with a smoldering bit of wood to represent the house. Adding a square on top for a chimney. Then X-ing in windows from top to bottom. Saying "Boom, boom, boom. Just like that."

"I'll be," said the kid.

"It makes sense, doesn't it? The sun rising and the reflections getting lower?"

"I never imagined a three-story house." Looking at the scratches that Hutchinson had made as if the drawing itself were the miracle, never mind the building they represented. The idea as astonishing as the thing.

"Imagine it now," said Hutchinson. Tomorrow we're going to go check it out. It's high time we had a change of scenery, don't you think?"

*

"So what do we do," Weller asked Patel, "besides hope Bud doesn't come back?"

"Oh, he won't come back."

"Then it's not our problem."

"Now, Henry. That doesn't sound like you."

He half ignored her, reaching over to tap at one of the gas gauges with a gloved finger. Its needle sprang to life, which seemed to satisfy him, and he turned back to Patel. "You're confusing me with somebody else."

"After all you went through."

"All I went through *for Penny*, you mean."

"You went places nobody would go. Nobody."

"For my daughter. For my family."

"You turned the whole world upside down."

"And look what happened," he said. "It went right back to the way it was."

"So?"

"So Ownership's still on top, and Black Rose still has all the firepower, and we're still hiding out just to stay alive."

"You didn't set out to change that."

"I know. I know I didn't."

"While I'll admit it would have been nice—"

Weller laughed. "It would have been *very* nice. And don't think there weren't moments when I hoped it would happen."

Patel looked him square in the eye. "So you wanted to save the world after all?"

"Only incidentally." He reached up to adjust a knob on the side of his helmet.

"And I'll bet you still do."

"Not while my wife and child are safe and happy. We're living in the closest thing to paradise we'll ever see, and we ought to make the best of it."

"What about Janey, then?"

"Janey?" Without thinking, he glanced at the bay adjacent to his. The empty bay where she usually worked.

"Janey's out there with Bud," she said.

"Janey and everybody else."

That's right," she said. "Janey and *everybody*. Out there with the virus that wiped out almost everything once before."

He opened the knob on the tank just a little. Signifying that he was ready for this conversation to be over.

"It's like you said, Henry. *She's out there with everybody else.* They're all at risk, all over again."

He chewed his lip. "And you think I should do something about it."

"We have something that nobody's ever had: a cure. A *cure,* Henry." She reached into the pocket of her coat and drew out a plastic bag sealed with a twist of wire. A finger-sized vial inside, just half full of a clear fluid. "We don't have much of it, though. But we do know how to make more. And we can share what we know with other people."

"Like who?"

"People who can make a difference."

"That doesn't tell me anything."

"Look, Henry," she said. "I still have some contacts at PharmAgra—"

"No way," he said, and with a snap of his head he clapped his visor down.

Twenty-Four:

Arrivals

They'd spotted the fire the night before, but they'd made no effort to protect themselves against whoever might have started it. Riders never came down here. Riders must have known that the landscape was poisoned, and chosen to save their energy for use in places with better prospects.

The dawn proved them correct. No figures on the ridgeline, no hoofprints in the grass, no passageways torn through the curtains of greenery. Above all no children dead in their beds, shot through the heart by the cruel crossbows of intruders come silently in the night. Just the morning, dawning as usual. Just the world.

The afternoon, though, was different. A harsh rustling through the kudzu. The slow clopping of hooves on the ground. A pair of voices calling out one to another, unafraid of announcing themselves.

"Whoever they are," Bud said to the old man who ran the place, "they ain't been here before. They don't know the way in."

"They're making their own way in," said the man. Cocking his head to listen as a long knife swept through stubborn vegetation. One time, two times, and then the sound of the hooves again. He said it once more, low. "They're making their own way."

The greenhouse's mossed-over walls and windows held them in a dense green darkness, so sound was all they had to go by. Any sunlight that came in came through in streaks and splotches and dappled streams from above, which didn't help. Just the sounds of men and horses. Or one man, at least. One man and either a woman or a child, given that there was one low voice and one higher. If there were more of them, they weren't talking.

"There's just the two," said Bud, the tension in his stance draining away.

"Unless that's what they want us to believe," said the man.

"Could be, I guess." Listening hard again. "Maybe they're scouts."

"Whatever they are, they *want* us to hear them."

"Or else they don't know we're here." Always the optimist, that Bud.

The man didn't move. "They know we're here, all right."

As if to prove him correct, silence fell in the green world. Nothing moved out there. Not so much as a breeze upon a leaf. Nothing moved inside, either. One silence responding to the other, for as long as it took.

At last: *"Easy, girl."* The man's voice and the squeak of leather on leather. A whickering from the horse. Or from the other horse. Or from some third or fourth mount, for all they knew. And then a clearing of the man's throat and finally a knock, knuckles upon the glass.

Bud started for the door, but the tall man took his shoulder.

"Please," he said. "I'm the host here."

*

Hutchinson rubbed his knuckles on the glass to work up a little clean spot that he tried looking through to no avail. Then he knocked again and waited. The boy coming up behind him quietly.

There hadn't been any people in the big house, so they'd come here. There hadn't been people, but there sure had been of signs of life. Plenty of them. They found indications of what looked like a couple of families living there or maybe just one great big one. Signs of little kids and bigger kids growing up. Bedrooms galore, with nicely made beds and drawers full of clothes. A neat kitchen full of cooking pots and dishes and so forth, clean as a whistle. What they hadn't found was a path from the mansion to the greenhouse. There must have been a back way, but they hadn't seen it, so they'd circled around a couple of times and ended up just cutting through the brush. The house certainly hadn't looked like a place where bandits or squatters or transients lived. It looked completely civilized and permanent, so they had been willing to go boldly up to the greenhouses and knock. Like two neighbors come calling.

The squeak of a door opening and the different squeak of it shutting again. Footsteps somewhere and then a tall man pushing back leaves and saying *can I help you?*

Just like that. "Can I help you?" And looking as if he meant it. His face was long and lined and serious, with a beard that began at his chin and ended there too. Like Abe Lincoln's beard, but gray and more or less untamed. The face of a patriarch above the beard of a prophet. He wore a farmer's overalls and he held the short handle of a three-pronged pitchfork as if it were required to complete his arm.

Hutchinson put out his right hand but the man didn't reciprocate. "My name's Hutchinson," he said. "This is Jim." Tipping his head toward the kid, still on horseback.

The man assessed him and the uniform he wore. "You're a long way from home, for Black Rose," he said.

Hutchinson smiled. "I'm a long way from Black Rose, is what I am."

The patriarch sized him up. Probably sizing up his relationship with the boy, too.

Hutchinson held a smile on his face and watched him think. Watching him come to his own conclusion. Imagining what scenarios the old man might be considering. He was too young to have retired from the service and too square to have gotten mustered out the way some did now and then. The old-timers and borderline crazies who lived rough on the periphery, working for whoever would have them.

"Riders haven't ever come down here before," the patriarch said. "Something go wrong? The boy sick?"

It would have been easy to agree, but Hutchinson didn't. The old man's theory made sense, because if anyone was more feared out here than Black Rose, it would have to be the Riders. More feared because they were more present. Right around the edges of daily life. Right up there on the ridge lines from time to time. A group of them could have overcome some Black Rose scout with no trouble, and then either taken his belongings or taken him whole for one of their own.

"Boy's fine," he said. "We ran off."

"Ran off from where."

"Places."

"Ran off from what, then."

"You name it," said Hutchinson.

The old man frowned. "Look," he said. "If you need something, you just say the word. Anything we can do for you, we'll do it. In the meantime, there's work to be done—and it isn't doing itself while I stand here talking."

"How about we pitch in?" said Hutchinson. "The boy and me?"

"That's all right," said the old man. Turning toward the door. Giving him a wary look that said outside the greenhouse was one thing, inside was another.

The boy, though. His eye fell again upon the boy and his whole manner softened. Something rising up inside him, maybe the impulse that had caused him to answer Hutchinson's knock in the first place. He paused and lifted his eyebrow with a kind of cautious curiosity. Was there something wrong with the boy? What if he was in trouble just being here, just traveling with this inscrutable individual in the Black Rose uniform? Kidnapped maybe. How could such a child ever hope to get away? Where could he go?

"The boy," he said at last. "He can come in."

Hutchinson looked at Jim. "Are you game?"

"Yes sir," he said.

Hutchinson smiled over at the patriarch. "It's your call, Pap. But I'm obliged to tell you—out of the two of us, he's the dangerous one."

The old man nodded as if he knew everything already, as if he understood the kind of jockeying and joshing that might go on between a man and a boy such as these two and how it might define whatever relationship they might have, and he waited for Jim to get down off the horse. He said he'd bring Hutchinson a little something to eat later on if he'd could use it, and then he ushered the boy off through the curtain of leaves.

*

Right off, Bud noticed how much the kid's backpack weighed. He saw how the kid tilted a little under the burden of it and how it sat like wet cement when he put it down on the long wooden table. You couldn't fool Bud.

The patriarch was asking the boy questions. Being reminded that his name was Jim. Apologizing for the way he forgot names at his age. He'd gotten out of practice, he said. As a rule he didn't have a lot of new names to deal with. Just this big family of his, and they'd always been here. This big family of children and grandchildren, each one of which he named off in descending order by age as if he were calling roll or predicting the order of their eventual deaths, pointing from one to the next. The only names he had to worry about were his own blood, he said, plus the occasional traveler like that old troublemaker Bud over there and what was her name again oh yes that would be Janey.

The kid didn't look to be starving, but the old man figured everybody out in the big polluted world was starving so this one must be too. Lunchtime was over but there was always more. Always more prepared and always more waiting, ripe and ready, right here in the greenhouse. He sat the kid down at the table and sent one of the younger ones off to the kitchen in the big house for anything she could pull together. Figuring there wasn't any point in asking what Jim would like because he'd like all of it.

The girl returned with one hot plate and one cold. On the cold one was raw everything, along with a puddle of something savory that the old man told him to scoop up and taste if he wanted. On the hot one was a triangle of mingled eggs and spinach and if it weren't cheese then it was something that passed for it, alongside sweet potatoes candied with honey. Jim dug in, not all that hungry until he got started. The potatoes in particular woke up something inside him. He'd never eaten anything half so sweet in all his life. He wanted to keep on eating them forever. He wanted to live forever just for that purpose.

"Good, huh?" said the old man. Looking as if he'd invented eating.

"Yes sir."

"You know what makes them so sweet?"

"No sir."

The old man pointed up toward the roof of the greenhouse, where part of one pane of glass had been cut away. Shapes were moving up there against the sun. Dark shapes as large as birds but bobbing and hovering. They jostled one another in a cloud of complex movement, and unlike birds they had weight to them that you could feel at this distance. Jim recoiled, putting down his fork. Like rats up there had learned to fly.

"Bees," said the old man. "They get bigger by the year. I suppose there must be some vegetation out there that favors such a change, assuming Mr. Darwin was right. Either that or some gene inside them got turned on and it doesn't want to turn off."

Jim looked down at his plate as if it had been poisoned.

"Don't worry, son. They don't have any interest in pollinating what we grow here. As for the honey—well, we don't seem to be getting bigger by the generation, do we?"

That seemed to satisfy Jim, and when he'd cleaned his plate the old man began to probe a little bit. He knit his brows and folded his hands and lowered his head on his neck just a fraction of an inch, saying, "According to your traveling companion, you're the tough one in the partnership."

Jim smiled. "He's kidding." And then, "Well, maybe not really."

The patriarch tilted his head.

Jim explained. Hutchinson in the tree. The poisoned dart. The ropes and the stretcher.

The story seemed to buoy the old man's spirits. "Never underestimate the power of youth," he said when it was done, his gaze drifting across the dim expanse of the hydroponic greenhouse, where youth largely of his own making labored on toward some unguessable future.

*

Bud showed up toward the end of Jim's story, planting himself alongside him and not far from that heavy backpack. Nodding like some old sage. "Black Rose ain't as tough as people might think, is how I understand it."

"Oh," said Jim, "they're tough all right."

Bud scoffed. "Hah. Ask them boys in Spartanburg how tough they are."

The old man spoke up. "Spartanburg?"

"That's where Janey and me just been."

"You didn't mention Spartanburg."

"They don't have nothing you need down there."

The man didn't pursue it. "Fair enough," was all he said. "Your business is your business."

Satisfied, Bud went on. "Spartanburg took down one little old helicopter God knows how long ago, and them Black Rose bullies never come back. Spooked but good. Like a bunch of little children."

The boy and the old man smiled at each other. Each of them deciding just to let him go on. Some people aren't worth educating.

Bud turned and squared up the kid's backpack on the table just to make sure it was as heavy as he'd thought, and once he was satisfied he called out to Janey. Invited her to come over and meet the new arrival like this was a party and he was hosting it. She came, but not in any hurry. She came lazily, reluctantly, as if some magnetic force were keeping her a certain distance away from Bud and sooner or later it would repel her altogether. She sat down next to the old man, on the other side.

"Janey here was born in Spartanburg," Bud said.

"The little town that whipped the world's mightiest paid army," said the old man. Not quite meaning it and hoping she'd understand that he had his doubts.

Janey caught on right off. "What's he been telling you?" she asked. "Bud likes to say a little more than his prayers."

The old man repeated the story he'd been told, while Bud himself sat across from him happy and satisfied. Smug, you could say. His story accepted and passed on and entered now into the world as truth.

Janey wasn't having it. "I wouldn't describe them as *scared off*," she said. "I'd say they made a strategic decision. We had the technology to bring down their copters, and we demonstrated it to everybody's satisfaction, and they decided we weren't all that interesting anymore."

"You could look at it that way," said Bud. "But I suppose the true measure of tough is a feller's willingness to go it alone." Looking at Jim but meaning to turn the conversation back to himself. "Ain't that right, kid?"

"Sure. I guess. My friend Hutchinson was tough enough to desert Black Rose, I can tell you that. He hated everything about 'em. Everything single they stood for. This one big raid they had up in the Northeastern Empowerment Zone? Killed all kinds of innocent people? Children even? After it was over he turned his back and walked clear. A person's got to be tough to do that."

Bud snickered. "If you ask them dead kids, he got religion a little too late."

The patriarch shook his head. "Better late than never," he said.

*

Janey found him with the horses. He had them tied up with their saddles off and he was brushing them down. Talking to them softly as if he'd done this kind of thing all his life and it came naturally. He heard her coming but he didn't quit. The horses flicked their ears in the direction of the rustling sound she made coming through the curtain of leaves, but he didn't give any sign at all.

"Your friend told us about what happened up north," she said. Thinking that that would be sufficient.

"You mean how he and his schoolmates nailed me with a poison dart, tied me down, and took me prisoner?"

"If he mentioned that," she said, "I didn't hear it. Sounds like fun, though."

He gave off brushing the horse. "It wasn't one of my proudest moments."

"Things happen."

"Things happen."

"What I meant," she said, "was that town up there."

He turned his attention back to the horse.

"What *used* to be a town," she clarified.

Hutchinson took a deep breath. "Another one of my not-quite-proudest moments," he said.

"There seem to be a lot of those."

"It happens," he said. "It happens when you stop and think about what you're doing instead of just doing it."

Janey went over to the other horse. She put a hand on its side and it didn't move away. If anything, it adjusted its weight slightly to return the pressure of her touch.

"I was there," she said. "In Connecticut."

"Then it's a miracle you escaped."

"I didn't have to. I was there just before, with the man you were after. With Weller."

"Henry Weller," said Hutchinson. "The guy who set all this in motion."

"You could say that."

"Tell me: do you know how he brought that big Chinook down?"

"He didn't," said Janey. "I did."

"Well bless your heart," said Hutchinson. And he put the brush aside.

Twenty-Five:

Portents

Penny told her mother: "She's coming back."

"Who, honey?" Thinking maybe she was talking about one of her classmates, somebody who'd been sick and had gotten better and was returning to school after an absence. "Who's coming back?" She looked over at Henry, thinking maybe he'd picked up some detail she hadn't. Some conversational fragment dropped earlier.

"Janey."

"Oh, I should hope not." Liz hadn't meant it to come out that way or at least not that quickly. "I mean, she's with that awful Bud, right? We don't want *him* around any more, do we?"

Weller sat before his oatmeal. Just listening.

"Bud won't be with her," Penny said. "I didn't see Bud."

Her father put down his spoon. "This was another dream, then."

"They're not dreams," Penny said. "They're real."

"I'm not so sure," said her father.

"Just wait," said Penny. "You'll see. She'll be back."

*

She made the same promise at school. All they had to do was wait a little bit and Janey would be back home in Spartanburg—minus that runner that everybody was so afraid of. Some of the children believed her because

160

they'd have believed anything. They'd have believed talk of magic or witch-craft or wizards. Some of the teachers believed her too, not because they were ignorant or because they were hopeful but because they'd heard that she'd been right about other things. How McCall had been bleeding inside, for starters. She'd called that one all right, long before he'd even gone to the infirmary. And she'd foreseen his recovery too. Plus there were stories about some dream she'd had where the earth was rising up against them and maybe that was true in a general way. Major Oates had closed the place down again and the whole world was arrayed against them, wasn't it?

There were others who confirmed her authority. Other children from Connecticut who remembered her first seizure or dream or attack or what-ever it was. The very first time, when her eyes had rolled back in her head and she'd called out, "It's on fire." Nobody knew what she'd seen then ei-ther, but they were pretty sure she'd seen something. Increasingly sure. Seen something in the dark of night back on the road, underneath the apple trees where they'd stopped for the night on their way here. Seen something that wasn't there but was someplace else instead. Maybe in the future.

It all seemed so long ago now. Long enough to have become a kind of myth.

Twenty-Six:

Departures

"Amazing," Hutchinson said, "how much change one person can bring about."

"One person and then another," Janey said. "First Weller, then me. And now there's this dude in there." Nodding toward the greenhouse.

"The old man? What's he got up his sleeve?"

"Not the old man. No. There's another one." She told him all about Bud. How he'd murdered his old partner as a way of poisoning all of Spartanburg. How he was running north now to get what he thought would be his just deserts.

Hutchinson shook his head with a kind of infinite sadness tempered by anger. "He's not one person acting alone," he said. "He's just a tool. A delivery system. The point of the spear. Believe me, I know all about guys like him."

"You used to be one."

"Right. But not anymore."

Janey thought for a minute. "He's still got more of that virus in his bag," she said. "Not much, but a little. In the syringe."

"A little is all it takes."

"No kidding."

"He got any plans for it?"

"I don't think so. I think it's just a souvenir."

"Some men love to collect souvenirs," Hutchinson said. "Trophies to mark the damage they've done. They used to call it *counting coup.*"

"Except in those days it was with scalps," she said.

"Scalps. That's right." Surprised that she would know such a thing.

"We were big on the history of war in Spartanburg," she said. "Between Colonel Marlowe and Major Oates." Offering it up almost as an excuse.

"It's always good to remember where we came from."

"I suppose."

"That's how we know where we're going. And more to the point, it's how we know when we've finally gotten ourselves headed in the right direction."

"Which would be?"

"Away from the past, instead of back into it." He told her maybe he was finally getting himself properly oriented. His transformation had played itself out in very clear stages, he said. First he'd done that long hitch with Black Rose, and then he'd gone through a moment of transformation when he'd decided to throw that conventional life away, and then he'd spent a while rootless and on the move. Going nowhere, really. Just going. Looking for anything that might present itself in the way of direction.

"And now you've found it?" she said.

"I think you've pointed it out."

She shrugged. "And it would be—?"

"The power of one person to set things in motion," he said. "I should have realized it a long while back, when I saw what Weller did, but I wasn't paying attention. I was still just part of a delivery system. I was still just the dumb-ass point of the spear."

"So what now?"

"Now I make sure that that fellow in there doesn't finish whatever mission he thinks he's on. I make sure that that syringe full of poison gets destroyed out here where it won't do any harm. Incinerate it. Bury the ashes. Make the world a better place instead of letting Ownership and Management keep making it a worse one."

"I'm in," said Janey.

"I thought I could count on you."

*

When Janey and Hutchinson came in, Bud shot them a look he'd have used on a couple of conspirators who'd been plotting against him in the open. Looking unhappy and outnumbered and about to be on the receiving end of something he didn't deserve. Like maybe he had one last chance to stand up for himself before the whole world shut down on him like a trap.

They just smiled back at him, Hutchinson especially, and that didn't seem to make him feel any more comfortable. Janey and the kid showing Hutchinson all around like he was everybody's long-lost pal.

"Where're you and the boy headed?" Bud asked when it came his turn.

Hutchinson was ready. "We thought we'd try our luck up north," he said. The kid looking at him from a little distance away and wondering what he meant, since north was exactly the one direction they weren't going. Janey catching the kid's eye and reassuring him without saying a word. The kid trusting her and trusting Hutchinson and not giving it another thought except to wonder what might be next. Some kind of adventure he hadn't counted on. He sure was glad he'd left home, where nothing ever happened.

They took off at daybreak. Bud leading the way and then Janey, followed by Hutchinson and the kid walking the horses. The horses carried everything for everybody, which wasn't much. The heaviest thing was Jim's pack with the gun in it. The horses moved at a pace they could have handled in their sleep, not stopping except for water at a stream they crossed and to crop some long grass that rustled beneath the shade of trees.

About sundown, a river. Too wide to cross here and too deep. They followed it for a while upstream at an imperceptible grade. The trees grew close on this side and they navigated among them, along a little narrow bank no taller than a man but grassed over and slippery. The ground on the opposite bank was flattened out. The trees had been stripped away a long time ago and over the years some brush had grown back. Not much. The earth was too compacted to yield readily. Man had made it over in his own stubborn and intractable likeness.

"That'll be a railroad line," Hutchinson said to Jim. "They ran them through the valleys, where things were already more or less level."

"I don't see any rails." Not as if he doubted Hutchinson, but because he wanted to learn something. See what he hadn't seen.

"I'd guess somebody hauled them off a long time ago. Cross-ties are gone too. They'd have been big old wooden staves, maybe eight feet long. Soaked in creosote and good for burning."

Jim looked hard and saw evidence. The wide flat pathway washboarded where the cross-ties had gone missing and the ground hadn't quite filled itself in. Gravel and dirt mixed together and uneven. He imagined people hauling those great wooden staves away in all directions, like ants bearing food.

They entered the woods after a while and made camp. Bud said they'd follow the river north for a couple of days until the railroad split off and then they'd follow the railroad. The railroad went to Washington and then to New York. Railroads always went somewhere. Rivers you couldn't be so certain about, since they wound and twisted and eventually came to nothing. That was the first lesson you learned out here in the woods. He parted with this information like some Indian guide from the ancient days. The night was coming on cold so they built a little fire. Jim unburdened the horses and walked them one by one back out to the river for watering. Returning to have his share of the dinner they had going. Everybody around the fire and getting sleepy.

Hutchinson licked his fingers and said he'd been relieved that Bud hadn't wanted to travel by night. He said he'd been led to believe that runners did that as a rule, but it was his opinion that going around under the cover of darkness was cowardly. He was glad he'd been proven wrong.

"You ain't wrong," Bud said, "but I ain't most runners." Grinning in the firelight.

"You operate on your own principles?"

"Not always. Lately, though, things have kind of shifted in my favor. I have reason to believe that I've come up in the world."

Hutchinson gave Bud back his grin or something like it. "I guess a fellow who's done what you've done, they'd roll out the red carpet anyplace you decided to go."

Bud looked over at Janey, who'd apparently told Hutchinson everything there was to know. Probably right down to the ticker tape parade he had in mind. She just looked back, steady and happy, as if every single fact of his life were already common knowledge. Seeing her that way put his mind at rest. It made him believe that Hutchinson was behind him entirely. In his thrall and under his command. *Imagine that*, he thought. *Imagine Black Rose looking up to a free agent like me.* It did more than put his mind at ease. It made him feel good. It made him feel better than ever, and that was saying something. "How about we drink to the red carpet?" he said. "How about we drink to my old partner McCall, God rest his soul, and to the warm welcome that's waiting for us in the big city."

He had a couple of bottles in his pack. He'd wanted Janey to carry some too, but she'd refused, so it was just the two. He hadn't touched a drop yet, although he'd been tempted. Now would be the perfect time, he said. They'd traveled a lot of miles and they'd put away a fine supper and they had this nice warm fire going. A little of that Johnnie Walker would help keep the chill from coming back. The kid could even have a taste. Little Jim. Why not? There wasn't a lot of Johnnie Walker Black Label left in the world, and he might as well get a sample of it while he had the chance.

"I'm not sure that's a good idea," Hutchinson said.

"Leave it to the military," said Bud, rising up and walking over to where the packs were slung around the base of a tree. "Rules and regulations."

"Not rules," said Hutchinson. "Just common sense."

Janey said Hutchinson was right. She said all Bud had to do was remember back a week or so to his own experience at the college, and he'd realize you shouldn't give that powerful stuff to a child. You shouldn't give it to anybody, was her opinion, but she wouldn't stop him from drinking it himself.

"You'd best not try," said Bud with a twinkle in his eye that was almost visible in the dark. Rummaging around in the packs underneath the tree. Apparently unable to find his own right off, much less zeroing in on one of the bottles he was after. A little time went by and he came back with the whisky and sat down opposite Hutchinson and unscrewed the cap. Tilted it back and drank. Rubbed the lip with the heel of his hand and gave the bottle to Hutchinson, saying "Go easy now. It ain't water."

Hutchinson put his lips to the bottle and tilted it back as if he were drinking, but he didn't drink. He just wet his tongue and that was enough. From across the fire Bud gave him an avid look that seemed to cover two separate things—a cunning hope that he would enjoy the whiskey and drink his fill, and a genuine delight to have opened the bottle again at last. To a man less on his guard than Hutchinson, it could have passed for a companionable look. A look of *we're in this together.* But Hutchinson had learned exactly what happened to individuals who threw their lot in with Bud. There was that syringe left in his pack someplace, after all. He might even have taken it out while he was getting the whiskey. With people like him, you had to be on your guard one hundred percent of the time. So he smiled as if he'd enjoyed the taste he hadn't quite had, and then he handed the bottle back.

*

McCall stumbled north. Leaving had been a lousy decision, and he knew it. But he also knew that he'd never get a shot at Bud by hanging around the car factory. And if he'd waited until he'd recovered completely, he'd never have caught the bastard. It was a long shot now, the odds were stacked so high against him as to be incalculable, but at least it was a shot.

He'd set out with a pack full of food and a pretty fair supply of water, but the food was too much to carry and the water didn't last long. He was thirsty as hell. All the time. Chalk it up to blood loss. Within a couple of days he'd jettisoned the food and drunk up all the water and he was out in the wilderness with nothing. Just his wits, which were dull, and his determination, which was strong but couldn't last forever.

He stayed close to water, and he drank freely whenever he needed to. He foraged for his meals and he ate whatever he found. Greens and fruits and berries that were probably time bombs of genetic disaster, their code winding its way even now into his DNA with the aim of killing him at some future date. He ate mushrooms and toadstools and tree-growing fungi that stood a fair chance of doing the job even faster than that. But he kept going. He made for a place he knew where an old sage and his children and his grandchildren grew good healthy plants in a hydroponic greenhouse, hoping both that he could get some decent sustenance and that Bud had stopped there as well and been delayed.

He went slowly, but he went steadily. And he kept his hope alive.

*

The bottle went around for a few more times than Janey thought was good for anybody. About halfway along, Hutchinson winked at her to indicate that she didn't have anything to be afraid of. She didn't take it the right way, though. She didn't know quite how to take it. There was a fifty-fifty chance that he was winking at her because the whisky had loosened him up. At least Bud hadn't pressed any on her or the kid.

The night drew on and the kid went to sleep in the waning firelight. Janey wanted to go to sleep too, but she didn't want to be next. She wanted to be the last if anything. She wanted to keep her eyes open until the last minute.

Bud held up the bottle against the stars and studied the whisky left in it. He started saying something about how the level hadn't gone down as much as he'd expected, but he stopped and kept his mouth shut. He'd been holding back too, not as completely as Hutchinson but as completely as he dared and desired, and he couldn't be sure of anything. Of who'd been drinking how much. Of what progress was being made toward what goal. The stars swam a little bit above his head, though, and the moon winked behind the cover of trees, and that was nice. He looked around the little clearing and saw a dark hump that was Jim sleeping. He pointed to him in the dark and said something about how giving the kid whiskey wouldn't have been much fun anyhow, to tell the truth it would have been just a waste of good whisky, and Hutchinson laughed as if what he'd said was humorous. Janey grunted. Either at Bud or at the two of them, nobody could say. Just being cautious. Just letting them know she was still awake and still making judgments.

After a while Hutchinson said he'd have one more taste of that Johnnie Walker and then he'd call it a night. Yawning and leaning up against a rock in the dying firelight with his eyelids drooping. Bud reached out the bottle to him more or less across the fire and Hutchinson reached out but couldn't make contact. Groaned once and said *well, shit* and fell back against the warm rock. Like he'd just given up. He threw his forearm over his face and that was it. Except that he wasn't asleep and he wasn't even particularly tired and he was determined to keep an eye on Bud for as long as it took.

Janey sighed and stood and went over to where the packs were. She found her own and pulled out a blanket and wrapped it around herself and came on back to the fire circle. Lying down pretty well where she'd started, nearer to Jim than to Bud or Hutchinson. Facing the fire and closing her eyes but not entirely. The whites of them still visible now and then from certain angles.

Bud didn't doze off either. He waited a while and had a few more tips from the bottle. He listened to hear if Hutchinson would start to snore, but nothing came. He shifted his weight and studied him where he lay, but Hutchinson was as still as one of the cooling rocks against which they'd all pushed themselves. The same went for Janey. He thought he saw a gleam from one of her eyes but he couldn't be certain. Above his head the stars still swam.

*

"I didn't think I'd ever see you again," said the patriarch.

"That means you've seen Bud."

"I have."

"He still here?"

"No sir."

"What kind of lie did he tell you?"

"He gave the impression that you turned on him."

McCall smiled like smiling hurt.

The patriarch smiled back and put his arm around him. "I didn't think there was much to it."

They went on up to the house. The day was late and in the looming shadows McCall looked like a ghost. Gray and ravenous and needful. Supper was just about ready, the smell of cooking coming down from the big house on a light breeze and the sound of voices coming down with it. Between the food and the family, McCall wanted to stay here forever. He caught himself thinking exactly that as they drew near and he sat down at a table alongside the old man. The idea startled him. He didn't remember feeling that way ever before. Didn't remember wanting to stay put. It wasn't like him, and it wasn't going to do either him or his cause any good now. This was the time for soldiering on. For staying in motion and overtaking that old partner of his and taking some kind of revenge. He didn't know what kind, exactly; he hadn't thought that far. And he didn't know for sure whether the revenge was for his own satisfaction or for the good of the world. His satisfaction and the fate of the world came to the same thing, if the object was stopping Bud.

He ate everything in sight. Speaking in a soft hoarse voice to the old man beside him about what Bud had done. How he'd accepted an offer from Black Rose—Black Rose paying their bills with AmeriBank scrip, so you make up your own mind as to whose idea it was—to wipe out the entire population of Spartanburg. How they must have slipped him the virus in a syringe and how he'd used it to infect McCall himself just out of pure meanness. In between bites he explained in that soft hoarse voice that Black Rose had made the offer to both of them in the first place. Half pay up front for poisoning a whole city full of people. The rest of the pay if you made it out alive, which they probably figured would never happen.

The old man nodded. "What I wonder," he said, "is how you were lucky enough to survive."

"I wasn't lucky. I was *cured.*"

"Then you didn't have the virus."

"I sure did. I was nearly dead inside a couple of days. I just about bled out through my own skin."

The old man shivered.

"Plus," McCall went on, "there's no way Black Rose would have paid Bud to deliver anything less than the real deal."

"I suppose you're right. So tell me about the cure."

"There's this doctor down there. She worked for PharmAgra in the old days. Genetic stuff."

"She produced a cure for the virus," the old man marveled. "Amazing."

"And here we'd all thought the virus was gone. Dead."

"Nothing that wicked ever dies," said the old man. "There's always somebody who'll keep it around, nurse it along just in case they need it."

McCall sighed.

"You know I'm right. Somebody kept the sample they gave to Bud, correct? And you can bet there's more where that came from."

"So even if I find him, and even if he's still got the syringe, and even if I manage to destroy what's in it a hundred times over, you don't think it'll make a difference?"

"Not for a minute. Not in the great scheme of things."

"It'll make a difference to me."

"*If* you catch him," said the patriarch. "And right now, you look like you need about a week's bed rest before you give it another try." And he spooned another helping of everything there was onto McCall's empty plate.

*

Hutchinson caught Bud with his hand in the cookie jar. He'd known he would. All he had to do was wait until he'd thought the rest of them were asleep.

Bud went creeping over to where their packs lay at the base of the tree. Nobody in the whole world had ever looked more suspicious than he did right then. Up on tiptoe and twitching his head around to make sure nobody was looking. Except everybody was, everybody except Jim.

Hutchinson heard him grunt as he lifted one of the packs. He knew it was Jim's he was lifting, no question. The weight of it and the grunting that indicated the weight were all the signs he needed. He knew what Bud was after, too. The gun, and why not. He already had a syringe full of poison, and now he wanted the only other weapon that presented itself. Some people can't have enough of anything.

Bud was distracted enough by the pack and the darkness and the drink that he never saw him coming. Hutchinson could still move with the commando stealth he'd learned in Black Rose, after all. It was something you never lost. You never lost that, and you never lost the knowledge you'd acquired of exactly how many ways there were to stop a man from doing something you didn't want him to do. Not necessarily to kill him, although that would always remain a possibility. You could always press a little harder on his windpipe or give his neck another fraction of a turn in the direction you already had it going. Such things are a matter of degree. You have to feel your way, you have to trust your senses.

The problem was that Janey didn't know how simple a thing this would be for Hutchinson, and since she'd been watching the whole business unfold she stood up and went over to lend a hand. Which caught the two men sufficiently off guard that they went down. All three of them in a heap on the packs, Janey at the bottom and then the two men on top, struggling. The gun slipping from Bud's hand and Hutchinson never loosening his grip on Bud's neck. Just trying to wrangle him into a spot where Janey could get up and get clear. Whispering in Bud's ear all the while. Advising him not to struggle since it was just a waste of energy. Telling him that the main thing he was after was that syringe. He hadn't decided what to do with Bud himself, but if he handed over that syringe and what was left in it he might go easy.

Bud went slack after a while. Windless and disoriented and saying *it's in my pack. It's right in the top compartment. Wrapped up in a rag.* He and Hutchinson working their way over to the dying fire and Janey picking up the pack and following. Rubbing at a spot on her arm where she'd fallen and gotten poked by something sharp. Thinking it could have been a million things—a folding knife or one of Bud's bottles of whisky or just some root sticking up—but afraid that it might not have been anything so plain or so benign.

The firelight showed that she was right. It wasn't the needle that had gotten her, though. It was the syringe itself, broken in the fall they'd all taken and ground into the flesh of her arm bearing its burden of poison on a thousand sharp shattered angles of graduated glass. She went weak and lightheaded. She had been through so much, and not one single bit of it had ever affected her this way. She'd always been proud of being tough, but she wasn't tough enough for this. No one could be tough enough for this. Tough enough to see it all end this way, out here in the wilderness, for all practical purposes alone. Everyone she cared about in Spartanburg already dead and her not even having mourned them.

They say that a dying person will see his life flash before his eyes, but Janey saw no such thing. What she saw was the life she had been deprived of. How the world had gone on while she'd spent her youth held captive in the car factory. How she'd sprung herself loose with Henry Weller only to return home again without seeing anything she could remember. And how this time she'd headed for the cities of the North only to die along the way. Despair brought her to her knees.

Not five feet away, Hutchinson had the gun pointed at Bud and Bud was busy searching his own pack. Hutchinson urging him to come up with that syringe or else. Bud saying it wasn't there. It had to be but it wasn't. Looking up at Hutchinson in the gloom and saying *honest I don't know where it's gone.*

Janey said, "I do." Showing them her arm. The blood on it looking black in the black night.

*

Hutchinson said, "Give her your jacket," and Bud gave it to her.

Then Hutchinson had him dig a hole and bury the broken glass in it. As much as they could find, along with the needle and the busted plunger and the rag that had held it all. Bud handling everything like it was deadly because it was. Asking out loud if Hutchinson wanted him to bury the backpack too. Just cover it all up. Hutchinson said yes. Deep.

Janey kicked dirt on what was left of the fire and saddled up the horses, conscious of the wounded arm inside the sleeve of Bud's jacket but resolved not to look at it again. As if not acknowledging it would make it go away.

The kid slept through everything.

Hutchinson took Bud into the woods with the gun aimed at his back. Bud with his hands in the air like it was comical even though it wasn't. Resigned and mocking. Janey watched them go, darkness into darkness. Waiting for a shot that didn't come.

He came out alone with the gun jammed into his belt and he woke up Jim. Said you ride behind me, Janey gets the other. Said we can't be more than a couple of days' ride from Spartanburg.

Janey asked why Spartanburg.

Hutchinson said he figured where else. Plus there's no place like home. Isn't that what people always said?

Twenty-Seven:

Reinforcements

Before this, Penny had never had the same vision twice. But now she had the worst one again. The one where she was dangling in the air high over the car factory, watching trouble come. Watching the earth rise up against itself and against everyone she knew or cared about. Inexorable waves of woe, like a live thing unfurling.

"It's coming," she said, "and there's nothing we can do to stop it."

Most people, even those who had come to place a certain amount of faith in her visions, believed that she was seeing something that had already happened. That she was dreaming of Bud and now Bud was gone and so her dream had no import other than as a reminder of the past. They told one another that her dream of an unfolding terror was correct, interpreted that way. There had been nothing they could do to stop Bud from poisoning Spartanburg, after all. You just had to remember that the dream hadn't told the whole story. They had been able to recover after all. To suffer the blow and shrug it off.

Besides, in the meantime she'd been dreaming of Janey's return. That was what she should focus on. Janey couldn't be arriving on that wave of ruin.

"Don't worry," one of her teachers told her. "Take it as a reminder that even if the worst imaginable things happen, people can rise up and move on."

"I'm not worried," said Penny. "You shouldn't worry about things you can't change."

"You're wiser than your years," said her teacher.

Penny didn't deny it. She'd been told such things before.

*

They more or less followed the trail that Janey and Bud had blazed north. Hutchinson and Jim in the lead on one horse, and Janey behind on the other. A rope between them thirty feet long. They did their best to make the horses keep their distance, Hutchinson and Jim wearing cloth bandanas over their faces in case the wind should shift.

By means of will, Janey stayed upright for most of the first day. She slept well enough during the first night, too, but when she awoke in the morning her strength was gone. She couldn't eat or drink. She couldn't climb back onto the horse. She felt split open and drained. Hutchinson held his breath and trusted his bandana and lifted her up with her bedroll and laid her across the horse's back. Then he threw off the jacket he wore and washed his hands in a sparkling creek near their campsite. Wondering what contagion he was sending where. Hoping they'd make Spartanburg by nightfall. Knowing it was impossible.

They came in sight of the mansion and the hydroponic greenhouses early in the afternoon, but Hutchinson was determined to give them a wide berth. Janey coughing where she lay facedown on the horse and blood spattering the dirt beneath the shade of leaves. Hutchinson wondering what on earth he was dragging across the face of the world and why. Whether he was just sowing destruction.

Jim watched the sharp rooflines of the greenhouses vanish once more into the woods. but before they were gone entirely he told Hutchinson they sure could use some extra food and fresh water. Janey in particular. Hutchinson said it was all he could do to keep them moving toward Spartanburg without the delay of stopping for food and water. Janey didn't say anything, and it was her silence that made him reconsider. The silence of her need.

Jim went alone. He'd had less physical contact with Janey and her belongings, so the duty fell to him. He rode off into the greenery while Hutchinson stayed behind and tied Janey's horse to a tree and kept his distance. Circling around and trying to ascertain anything he could as to the particulars of her condition. He drew a little nearer and told her the kid was going for water in case she hadn't heard, or in case she'd heard but hadn't quite understood.

She seemed to rouse up a little at the idea of water, although he couldn't be certain. There was a canteen slung from a rope around her horse's neck, and Hutchinson couldn't say when she'd drunk from it last. He'd been afraid to come close enough to press it on her. He wouldn't let the kid do it either. He hated himself for his cowardice and self-interest, but the hatred didn't abate the fear. He told himself that he didn't dare get too close because getting too close risked everything. He was all she and the kid had to count on to get them to Spartanburg.

He stood on his toes and pulled down some big leaves and used them like a potholder to take hold of the canteen. She stirred at his proximity. He could barely bring himself to look at her. Her face and arms were bruised and bloody, beginning to leak from within. Her tongue was swollen and it got in the way of what little water was in the canteen when he tipped it up for her. He wept and put down the leaves and held her face in his hands so that she might drink.

*

The kid came back with reinforcements, if you could call one man reinforcements.

McCall.

Stronger for a couple of days of rest, and raised up like Lazarus to walk the earth again. To run, really, given how he tore through the leafy green with Jim at his heels. A sack of food slung over one shoulder and a bladder of water over the other, but moving almost as if he carried no load at all.

"You must be Hutchinson," he said as he tossed him the sack. Hanging the water around the neck of the horse and then moving on to Janey. He was fearless in the presence of the virus, and his careless bravery would have shamed Hutchinson if he hadn't been ashamed enough already.

"The kid says you're bound for Spartanburg," McCall said. "Smart move. There's a doc down there cured me."

Hutchinson didn't question it. He just snugged up the rope around the horse's neck and said, "We'll get her there just as fast as we can."

"I can give you some directions," McCall said. "I'd take you all the way myself, but I've got another little problem that needs attention."

"I understand."

"The fellow who got this mess started."

"Bud?" said Hutchinson.

"That's right. Bud. What do you know about him?"

"I know there's one little problem that doesn't need your attention anymore."

And so the four of them headed out together.

*

They traveled through the rest of the day and on through the whole night and into the next day without pause. McCall on foot leading Janey's horse. Every step painfully slow. Eating and drinking on the fly except when they had no alternative but to water and graze the horses. Janey had no appetite, but McCall sloshed some water into and around her mouth from time to time as best he could. Talking to her softly, saying he was sorry for what Bud had done to her but he'd done it to him too. They had that in common. Telling her that all they had to do was get back to Spartanburg and Doc Patel would fix her right up.

He kept up a stream of talk as constant and comforting as moving water, and when at a certain point in the deep middle of the night she quit responding by even so much as an occasional twitch he decided that she was asleep. It beat the alternative. He kept talking anyhow. Telling her that Spartanburg wouldn't be far now. Not far at all.

*

Penny saw them first, and it wasn't even in a vision. The teacher had taken her class up on one of the elevated catwalks that overlooked parts of the car factory for an outing among the high windows that was as close as they'd get now to a nature walk—and through the north-facing windows she spied the horses coming out of the trees. Two horses and three people. No. Not three people. Four people.

"It's McCall on the first one," she said. "With Janey." How she had identified that pale and limp figure may have been attributable to one kind of vision or another. Either way she was correct, and soon everyone knew it.

The children came clattering down the iron stairs bearing the news with them, and a call went out for some kind of authority, and both Patel and Oates responded. Everyone else came too. Everyone who'd feared Bud's return and now wondered what Janey's homecoming would bring.

Oates played it safe the way he'd been playing everything, acting as if the decision weren't his. As if this little closed-off compound were a democracy. "What do you folks think?" he said, standing among them in the open area under the high windows. Knowing that the people who mattered—the ones who knew what his will was without his even having to say it—would speak up and set the right things in motion. Which they did. Stating opinions like "Closed-up works just fine with us," and, "If folks go outside, they take their chances."

Oates frowned and nodded like some old justice weighing evidence. Seeing their point and letting everybody else know that he agreed with the wisdom of it.

A hammering came from outside. Fists on a locked door. A muffled voice that probably belonged to McCall, calling out.

"He went outside," somebody said. "He made his choice."

Oates nodded once, twice.

"Same goes for her." Meaning Janey. It went without saying.

"I guess we're in agreement, then," said Oates.

Dr. Patel came forward. "Unless you think we have an obligation to do right by other human beings," she said. Passing through the throng to approach Oates where he stood. There was a challenge in her dead-serious look and another challenge in the effortless way the crowd parted for her.

"Doing right?" Oates said "I think we all agree that looking after your own people is a pretty good place to start doing right."

"It's *Janey*. She's one of your own."

Oates raised an eyebrow and sighted down his nose at Patel. "She is. You, on the other hand, are not." At which an audible shock passed through the crowd. The sound of people choosing up sides.

The hammering didn't stop.

"We have a cure. One dose. We can save her."

"They'll all be infected."

"Probably," she admitted.

Oates laughed. *"Probably,* says the doctor who ought to know. Are you peddling hope now, instead of science?"

"All right. They'll all be infected. Certainly McCall, if it's true that she's been riding with him."

"Fine. So we take Janey in, and we turn the others away?" Shaking his head at the obvious cruelty of it. Other people shaking their heads too. Some of them looking as if whatever faith they'd once had in Patel had crumbled to dust right then and there.

"Unless," she said, raising a finger for attention, "unless he got some immunity with the drug."

"But we still turn him loose. And what about the other two. What are they to think?"

The hammering on the door went on unabated. Whoever was pounding out there had plenty of energy, that was for sure.

"I don't know," she said, resigned. "I don't know what they'll think. But I suspect they came to get help for Janey, more than for any other reason. So I think they'll understand."

Oates chuckled. "You have great faith in human nature."

"And you don't," she said with a smile. "The two of us are different that way."

People nodding. The tide of opinion turning, if only just a little.

The hammering and the shouting outside going silent for a minute.

"And here I thought you only had faith in science."

"I have faith in the future," she said. "You, on the other hand—"

He gave her a condescending look, a look that nearly stopped her. But not quite.

"You," she said, "have faith in the past. In shutting down instead of opening up. In protecting the *status quo* instead of moving forward. Nothing ever gets any better that way, *Mr.* Oates."

At which instant came the sounds of gunfire and breaking glass.

Twenty-Eight:

Spillover

Gunfire and breaking glass will put people to a test. Even though everybody knew it was Janey out there along with McCall and a couple of others, a man and a harmless-looking young boy, most of them scattered like rabbits. Most of them but not all of them.

Weller, who'd been on the periphery because he'd been late to come out from his post in the machine shop, was the first into the hallway. He only got so far. He stopped when he saw light spilling in from the broken window and he pushed himself against a wall to sidle closer little by little, waving back the handful of people who'd followed behind him. Patel and Oates and some others. He went carefully forward, keeping a turning in the hallway between himself and whatever. There was a voice from down there but he couldn't make it out. A voice that didn't sound like McCall.

Then there was more breaking glass. More breaking glass but no more gunfire. A sound of metal scraping and glass falling. Weller put his head around the corner and saw a hand wrapped in a bandana in the shattered window, using the gun to push out what was left of the safety glass and reinforcing wire. Then the gun disappeared and the hand came in again, reaching down for the knob.

Oates' voice came from behind him: "Who was in charge of sealing that door, anyway?"

But no one answered. No one had to. He wasn't *Major* Oates anymore.

Weller stepped around the corner, and Patel followed him. The man with the gun threw open the door and pressed his back against it to let the air and the sunlight pour in, and McCall stood behind him with Janey in his arms. Stepping forward now, over the threshold, with a pleading look on his face. "You folks wouldn't turn her away," he said.

"You know how to get to the infirmary," Patel told him. "I'll meet you there in five minutes."

McCall slipped down the hall with Janey in his arms. Oates put a protective hand over his nose and mouth as the pair of them passed, and faded back without a word into an open workroom. Leaving Weller to stand his ground before Hutchinson and the kid, undecided as to what ought to happen next. He looked at the road-weary pair of them and believed that in spite of the intruder's gun, it was going to be his call.

*

The infirmary felt almost like home to McCall. He lay Janey down on the same table where he'd lain for the days of his sickening and the days of his perilous recovery. She was all but unconscious every moment now. Not drifting in and out, but just adrift. He found a white sheet in a cabinet and pulled it over her wasted body and watched patches of red appear through the cloth where it touched her, and he wondered if she were really in her body at all anymore. In that poor sad deflating sack of flesh and bone.

He drew water and brought it to her lips, but she made no response. He looked helplessly at the intravenous setup, the rubber hoses and the bottles and the needles, and he figured that that was the only way they'd ever get fluids into her. If they could pierce her vague skin and find something like an intact vein to feed.

He stood by her, waiting for Patel, and as his eyes focused and refocused he caught his own reflection in the glass window of a cabinet beyond the examining table. Even to himself he looked ghostly. His skin didn't seem to fit anymore. It was too big for what was left of him. He spied a medicine chest with a glass mirror on the front of it and he went over for a closer look. His hair and his beard were colorless and he'd sunken behind them. If you had asked him if the figure in the mirror could have made the journey that he'd just made, he'd have denied it. He'd have told you that that poor soul couldn't have made it up a flight of stairs. And yet here he was. Here he was pitying Janey on account of her condition and fearing for her life, when his own was still so fragile.

He gave himself one last appraising look. Thinking about how much power the human spirit might actually possess and wondering about how small a spark might be all that was necessary to bring a person back from the edge. Then he turned away and went to the door and waited for Patel. She wouldn't be long now. She couldn't be. Janey couldn't endure much more.

*

The man with the gun said, "How about at least we water these horses?" He was still standing in the doorway. The kid behind him had both leads in one hand.

"Feel free," said Weller. Indicating the world outside with a tilt of his head and taking a step forward. "There's plenty of water. A whole irrigation system." He didn't say he'd designed it himself and built most of it, but there was a kind of pride in the statement that was unmistakable. As if he'd already thought of every single that might happen ever. Even this. Their arrival and their need.

Hutchinson still held the door open with one hand, and he slid the pistol back into his belt with the other.

Weller watched it go. "You won't be needing that," he said.

Hutchinson smiled. "I was just using it for a glass cutter." Folding the bandana and jamming it into his pocket. "That damned wire-reinforced safety glass," he said. "It didn't give easy. And we were in kind of a hurry."

Weller went past Hutchinson into the sun and tilted his head to show the kid what direction. The cultivated fields around the car factory had gone wild again quickly. Nature had moved back in. Weller walked down rows that weren't exactly rows anymore. Leading the way around the east side of the building, and the others followed with the horses. The kid keeping pace but Hutchinson lagging behind.

Weller looked at the kid. "What's with your father?" he said. "He's the one who wanted to water the horses in the first place."

The kid stopped and looked back and scratched his head. "He ain't my father," he said. "He's just somebody I know."

"Either way, he ought to try keeping up." Weller took the kid by the shoulder and pointed him toward a little tin shed a few yards away. "Water'll be over there," he said. "Turn the big red wheel. There's buckets around and what have you. A couple of basins. You'll figure it out." And then, as the kid and the horse moved on, he headed back to see what was keeping the man with the gun.

"I don't know about horses," he said when he found him, "but that one doesn't look so good."

"Let's hope she's only dehydrated," said Hutchinson.

*

The needle went in easily. Patel told McCall it would have been better if she had been able to locate a healthy vein with good blood flow, but then again if Janey had possessed healthy veins with good blood flow she wouldn't have needed the drug. So you took what you could get. The skin of Janey's upper arm was soft beneath the needle and the muscle beneath it gave easily and Patel steadied her thumb on the plunger. She pushed it in slowly, imagining the drug pouring into a rushing river of blood that would carry it everywhere in the young woman's body, but knowing that the best she could hope for would be a kind of blooming out into a sluggish pond. It almost seemed like a waste of the last bit they had.

But you never knew.

"Was I this far gone?" McCall asked. Standing alongside the table with not the slightest bit of protection between himself and Janey, because why start now?

"No. She's had a few days' head start on you. It's made a significant difference."

McCall shook his head.

Patel withdrew the needle and checked the syringe and disposed of it, a little sadly.

"It'll be a miracle if she recovers."

"I'm not sure there's any such thing as a miracle, Mr. McCall."

"I guess you'd know."

Sorry for dooming his hope, Patel attempted a smile. "On the other hand," she said, "this certainly would qualify." And then she stepped toward the door, leaving the two of them behind. The one who had suffered and the one who suffered still.

*

Weller kept his distance from the horse and from the man too. The man who identified himself as Hutchinson and said he wasn't Black Rose anymore despite his Black Rose uniform, just a wayfaring stranger. A runaway keeping company with that other runaway, the boy, Jim.

Weller said maybe Hutchinson remembered him. Or remembered hearing about him. He was the one who'd made that deal with Anderson Carmichael, the richest man in the world, involving Black Rose training and a certain fancy car he'd more or less liberated from this factory right here.

"You're kidding me," said Hutchinson.

"I am not." Walking along toward the tin shed where the kid was watering the first horse. Letting Hutchinson and the other horse keep their own pace behind him.

"So I've found you at last."

The words startled Weller. The man had a gun, after all.

"I've been right here."

"I wasn't looking here. I was looking in the Northeastern Empowerment Zone. Old Connecticut." He stopped at the end of the rope to let the horse catch up. Ahead of him Weller stopped too. The horse barely moving now. "Come on, old girl," Hutchinson said. "Let's get you some water."

"You must have just missed me. Back in the Zone."

"Right. You made some enemies, pal. When you wrecked that car and all."

Weller nodded.

"I can't say I blame you for hiding out down here in the boondocks."

"I haven't been hiding out."

"No?"

"No. I've been living my life. Besides, what was even *left* up there, once you people got through?"

"Less than you might think," said Hutchinson. "That's why I quit. It all got out of proportion. When you weren't there, they killed everybody that was left. Hundreds of them. Like bugs. Everybody they could find. And they burned the whole town to ashes."

Weller said, "I'd have stayed around if I'd known."

"You'd have stayed around and gone up against Black Rose. Right." Laughing.

"Really. I would have, if it would have saved everybody else."

Hutchinson quit laughing. "Everybody's a hero after the fact," he said. "Even me."

"Honest," said Weller. "I think I'd have sacrificed myself if I'd known. Let them have me. Let *you* have me."

"It's easy to think so." That was all he had to say on the subject. He did talk to the horse, though, softly but with insistence. "Come on, old girl," he said. She had quit moving altogether. She just stood resolute, her legs stiff as pokers, every joint locked. Not even bending to crop the weeds, although she must have been starving.

Up ahead, the kid stood alongside the tin shed waving an empty bucket in the air. Banging it with his free hand and hurrying them on. The horse was behind him, bent forward, neck down, avidly drinking.

Hutchinson tugged at the lead.

"I don't think she's coming along," said Weller.

"She's been doing fine. It was a hard trip, but she's been doing fine up till now."

Weller shook his head. Hutchinson gave another small tug and then began to walk toward the horse, coiling the rope as he went. Weller put out a hand as if to stop him but not quite doing it, since stopping him would require contact. "I think I'd leave her be," he said. Taking one step back and then another.

The kid gave off banging the bucket, and a look of alarm passed across his face. He dropped the bucket to the ground and checked behind him to see that the horse was still drinking and then he started toward them at a run.

Hutchinson let go of the rope to catch him as he flew past. "Whoa up there, Jim." The two of them struggling a little as the kid tried to free himself to run and Hutchinson did his best to save him from the danger buried in his own kindest instincts. Instincts that had been bred in him from the day he was born, way out there in the Piedmont with the rest of the Riders, dependent on horses for every single thing.

Weller asked, "You ever see an animal get the virus before?"

"No." Then, to the kid, "How about you? You've been around horses."

"No sir." Still struggling a little, but less. "I never seen one get the virus."

The horse coughed and Weller took another step back. "I believe we're seeing one now," he said.

Twenty-Nine:

Recovery

Weller was in the machine shop, hammering at a crescent of iron and studying it up close and frowning and hammering at it again, when Patel stopped by on her way between the infirmary and the lab.

"I guess you got your wish," she said.

"What wish would that be?"

She reached into her pocket and pulled out a plastic bag he'd seen before. The bit of twisted wire that had kept it shut was gone, and the vial inside was empty. "There's nothing to take north anymore," she said. "I gave the second dose to Janey."

"And?"

"And I don't know. It might be too late."

Weller studied the iron before him and struck it once, hard.

"I hope it's not too late, Henry. The drug could still take hold. It could still work."

"And if it doesn't?"

"If it doesn't, we'll lose Janey. And we'll know one of the drug's limitations."

"If it does, though? If it does take hold?"

"We'll know more about just how powerful it might be."

Weller hammered again.

"Actually," she said, "we'll know more about how powerful it *might have been*. If we'd been able to manufacture more of it. If we'd had the materials and the backing."

"You mean if I'd taken it north the way you wanted me to."

Patel shrugged. "Done is done, Henry."

He put down the hammer. "If I'd taken it, and then she'd shown up here with the virus, she'd be dead already. Look at it that way. I have saved her."

She put the bag back in her pocket. "And look how much protection the rest of us have now," she said. And then, as she turned for the door, "There's still a way, you know."

*

Day after day, McCall stuck by Janey as if he'd been the one responsible for infecting her. He never left her side except to clean himself up, and he didn't go far to accomplish that—only to the ruined little decontamination shower that Janey had doused Weller in when he'd first arrived and they'd taken him for a threat from the outside world. It was an automatic system that sprayed some kind of chemical disinfectant that made his skin burn like fire before it switched over to cold water that did the opposite. First fire and then ice, two ways the world might end. He supposed he could have gone back to his old quarters to clean up, but he didn't try. Somebody might have stopped him and tried to keep him from entering into the general populace. He might have gotten involved in something that would have kept him away from Janey's bedside for who knows how long. And he might have missed the moment when she finally opened her eyes again, if she ever did. As for meals, Patel and the medics brought them. Surely hoping that sooner or later Janey would have an appetite too.

Outside the walls of the car factory, the kid stuck by the dying horse in the very same way. He camped in the field by her side. Bringing her buckets of water that she ignored and clumps of grass that she didn't even sniff. He didn't touch her, though. He knew better than that. And he stayed upwind as best he could. She and the other horse were all the connection that remained to the place he'd come from, and he had a responsibility to her and to everything she meant. So he kept vigil in spite of his native caution, and nobody could talk him out of it. They all tried. Patel tried a science angle and Weller tried a kind of fatherly reason and Oates came out all alone when nobody was around and bellowed at him flat-out, as if he were still the old Major Oates and Jim were the rawest recruit. All to no avail whatsoever. The boy would not be moved.

*

They isolated Hutchinson in the infirmary, since he hadn't isolated himself the way the kid and McCann had done. The medics brought him meals and took his vitals and drew blood once a day as if they knew what to do with it. They kept an IV set up just in case. But he didn't show any signs of infection as the days went by. He actually got healthier, since he was eating regularly and he wasn't out in the elements. Dr. Patel said maybe another week or two and they'd let him out. He didn't complain about captivity. He just asked about the kid and the girl and the horses, and as long as he got regular reports he was satisfied, even though the reports about the one horse were bad and the reports about the girl were oblique.

*

By and by the drug took hold in Janey's system. McCall watched it happen. He watched it and he kept notes that he shared day after day with the medics, since his observations were far more detailed and accurate than their own. He noted every twitch of a nerve, every intake of breath, every flicker of life behind either pale eyelid. At first his observations made no impression on the them. But as the days passed and the volume of proof grew instance by tiny instance, they began to pay attention. Patel took notice as well, although she didn't quite dare accept the evidence of McCall's senses—or even her own. The odds were too long and the stakes were too high. Trying to look squarely at something you cared so much about was nearly impossible. And yet by the end of the first week, anyone could have seen the change.

*

Patel told Weller, "She's on the mend."

He smiled behind his welding helmet. "You're a miracle worker," he said.

"I *was* a miracle worker. It was my great shining moment."

"I know, I know. And it could have been mine."

"It's still possible," she said. "If you want it to be."

Thirty:

Weller's Return

The kid came to the door crying. As tough as he was, in the end he was just a kid. Just a kid a long way from home and with nothing to cling to. Only a stranger he'd run off with and a weak horse that was tied up next to a tin shed and another horse that had finally drawn its last breath. He'd had to back away from it at the end, there'd been so much blood. The ground was saturated with it. He'd had to watch at some remove while one of the last links to the world he knew slipped away for good.

They took him straight into the infirmary and put him in the examining room next to Hutchinson's. All three rooms were taken now. Janey and Hutchinson and the kid right in a row. It was a good thing that Janey was improving and the other two weren't getting any worse, because they were strictly at capacity. Housing capacity if not treatment capacity. They'd gone well past treatment capacity a long while back.

He was still sobbing when they locked the door behind him. Hutchinson heard. He spoke to him through the wall, his voice raised louder than he wanted it to be raised since he knew Janey was on the mend in the room on the other side. If she was sleeping he didn't want to wake her, but the kid needed consolation. Finally he realized that these examining rooms hadn't been meant for isolation in the first place. They had drop ceilings, big white panels that lifted right up. He rolled the examining table over to the wall and raised a panel and climbed. Figuring the kid hadn't had the comfort of a parent in a long time if ever, and maybe he wouldn't mind whatever clumsy attempt a person like him could make in that area

*

Dr. Patel was the one who found them together. She'd heard about the kid's reentry and figured there was no reason to treat a poor child as cruelly as all that. To let him inside and then lock him up. Not when he was show-ing no signs of the virus, and when Hutchinson had been clean all week as well. Nobody that she knew had ever established an isolation protocol for people exposed to the virus, but a week was probably as good as anything. Especially when there was an innocent child involved.

They were seated together on the floor, communing as if they were warming themselves around a campfire someplace. The boy talking and the man listening. Nodding his head and making sounds of accommodation the way a person will when words won't do. He didn't even look up when Patel unlocked the door and swung it wide and came in, although the boy looked up. He looked up and she saw his face and she was struck by the woe in it.

"The horse—" said Hutchinson.

"I know," said Patel.

Hutchinson crumpled his lips in a frown that was apologetic and be-seeching at the same time. "Jim and that horse go back a long way," he said, reaching out to touch the kid's shoulder and coming slowly to his feet. He hadn't had much in the way of movement for the past week, and everything was stiff.

The kid hung his head.

Hutchinson moved closer to Patel. Close enough that he could speak to her softly and be heard but not by the boy. "I'd like to handle the burial," he said.

She thought that would be a fine way to commit suicide, and she told him so. But not so the boy could hear.

*

Over supper with Patel, Hutchinson kept up his insistence on burying the horse. The crowd in the diner was thinner than usual thanks to him. Everybody knew everybody in Spartanburg, and even though Hutchinson had been isolated since he'd arrived they all knew who he was by default. Patel brought him in and sat alongside him as a vote of confidence. A few people who'd been getting ready to eat slid as far away as they could, but not all of them. If he was all right with Patel, he was probably all right.

They'd brought Jim too, and she found a spot for him with a group of children who studied him as if he were some kind of wild animal they'd like to bring home and tame.

"I have a duty to that boy," Hutchinson said while he and Patel waited for their dinners to arrive. "And a duty to that horse."

"We all have duties to one another," she said. "There are always a variety of ways to fulfill them."

He shook his head. "There's no reason for me not to do it."

"There's the virus."

"If I didn't get it already, maybe I won't get it ever. Maybe I'm immune."

"I doubt that." Watching the counterman come out of the kitchen with their plates.

"But you don't *know.*"

"I don't *know.*" Unfolding her napkin.

He dug in. "Fine," he said, through a mouthful. "We can't just leave her out there on the ground, so the sooner I get started, the better."

She ate a little. "What I think we ought to do is incinerate the remains," she said at last. "It would be cleaner."

"No," he said, "it's not decent. And besides, if I do catch something, you'll just give me the same drug you gave the girl. It works like a charm."

"I'd be happy to," said Patel, "if we had any more of it."

Hutchinson looked up from his plate. "You're out?"

"Completely out."

"But you can make more."

"No. That's it. We're strictly on the defensive from here on in."

Hutchinson took a bite and chewed for a minute, thinking. "All right," he said. "I'm going anyhow. I'll need more than a shovel, though. A lot more."

"Go see Henry Weller in the morning," she said, resigned. "He works in the machine shop."

"Will do."

"And if fooling with that horse doesn't kill you, I might have another project for you when you're done."

"What's that."

"Heading north. Back to New York. With instructions for making the cure in quantity."

"No good," he said.

"You could save the world."

"I'm a Black Rose deserter. They'd shoot me on sight. You'll have to find yourself another volunteer."

"I've been working on one," she said.

"Who'd that be?"

*

"You'll forgive me if I don't lend you a hand out there," Weller told Hutchinson the next morning.

"You don't need *my* forgiveness."

"I guess not." Leading him down a concrete passageway to an low-ceilinged garage where they kept certain semi-retired equipment. A little bucket loader that must have been used to maintain the blacktopped parking lots once upon a time. A bulldozer that nobody had any use for anymore.

The loader started right up, and Weller adjusted the choke. "You sure about this?" he hollered over the noise of the engine. "About going out there? Messing with that thing?" Idling the engine down and climbing out of the cab.

Hutchinson was tying a bandanna over his nose and mouth. "I'm sure. The body's got to be disposed of. And I owe it to her."

"Better you than me."

Hutchinson laughed behind the bandanna. There wasn't any humor in the sound of it. "Are you the same Henry Weller who once went up against the whole world and came out on top?"

"I am."

"The same Henry Weller who'd have sacrificed himself to Black Rose if he'd had the chance?"

Weller nodded more or less to himself, going off to work on the chains and padlocks that kept the garage door shut against the outside world.

Hutchinson just shook his head. "I guess things change," he said.

And then he fired up the loader and headed out.

*

"I don't know what's become of me," Weller said. He said it to himself out loud in the echoing garage, and he whispered it to himself quietly behind the screen of his welding helmet, and when the day was over and Penny was tucked into bed he said it straight out to Liz. "I don't know what's become of me."

"What are you talking about?" She looked at him with real and immediate concern, as if he'd just complained of some illness that had all but overwhelmed him. Something he'd been keeping a secret but couldn't keep a secret any longer. "Are you feeling all right?"

"I feel fine," he said. "I just don't feel like myself anymore. I haven't felt like myself in a long time."

"I don't—"

"I feel…confined. Pent up."

A look passed across Liz's face that suggested she'd seen this coming from a long way off.

"You used to say you wanted to go home."

She nodded.

"You still feel that way?"

"I don't know." Ransacking her mind and her heart. "I honestly—."

"How about Penny?"

"Penny's happy."

"She doesn't talk to you about going home?"

"Why should she? This is home now."

"Not to me, isn't. Not yet. And not ever, I don't think."

She reached out a hand and took his forearm. "If it'll make you happy, we'll go back."

"That's the thing. There's nothing to go back to." And he told her what he'd learned from Hutchinson. What Black Rose had done.

"If he was in charge of that platoon," Liz said, "then he's responsible."

"No." Withdrawing his arm from where she held it. "I'm responsible. I'm responsible for everything. You said it when we left home, and you've said it since, and you've been right. The whole thing. I caused it."

She tried reading his face, but it was impossible. After all these years she couldn't decide whether what was behind it was guilt or woe or a strange kind of stubborn satisfaction.

"If I hadn't left home with Penny," he said, "there'd be a couple thousand more people breathing on this earth right now. People we knew. And a million other things wouldn't have been disrupted. Dr. Patel's work. That kid from the Riders who's out here all alone with nothing left and nobody to turn to. Janey and McCall who got sick. And the rest of us who still might."

"Done is done," she said.

"This isn't the world I wanted, Liz."

"You have to deal with the world as it is."

"We're locked up like prisoners. We're afraid of everything."

"It's not that bad. I'm happy enough. Penny's happy."

"Penny doesn't know what she's missing."

"Henry."

"I can fix it, honey. Dr. Patel's been after me to fix it for a long time."

"You can't *fix it*. There's nothing to fix."

"I can go north. I can share the cure for the virus with the whole world. And then I can come back, and we can open this place up again."

"Why you?"

"Because every life I can save by spreading the cure is one life I've atoned for."

"You don't need to atone for anything."

"I do, Liz. Besides, think about Penny. I moved heaven and earth to get her sight back, and then I let them away everything there was to see."

"Henry."

"I'm going to make that right," he said. "I'm going to fix it."

Thirty-One:

Out

Oates, leaning up against the door of Dr. Patel's lab in his overalls, said, "They tell me we're out."

"Out of what." Not even looking up.

"The drug. The cure. I hear there isn't any more of it."

"You've heard correctly. There were two doses. That's all."

"How come? How come there were only two?"

"That's all the raw material I could come by. The mail order supply companies aren't exactly in business anymore."

"Is there any more at the college? We could send somebody."

"No. There's no more."

Oates put his hands in his deep pockets and leaned back against the doorframe. "Then I guess it's up to me," he said.

"You'll go?"

"Go?" he said. "Where would I go?"

"To New York. Take the formula. Make peace with Ownership, with Black Rose, with everybody. Because you'll have the cure that they've never been able to produce on their own."

Oates frowned.

"You'll come back a bigger hero than ever."

Oates frowned some more, but there was a light somewhere behind his eyes.

"If anyone has the courage to face those people, it's you."

"They'd never believe a word I said. And some Black Rose sniper would murder me before I got a syllable out."

"That's a chance you'd have to take. One more reason you'd come back a hero. With a better story to tell than anything you and Marlowe ever cooked up."

"No," he said, taking his hands from his pockets and standing up straight in the doorway. "It's useless."

"Then what did you mean when you said it was up to you?"

"I meant I'd have to do a hard thing that I've done before. Lock everything down completely."

"We're pretty well locked down now."

"We can do better than *pretty well*. I'm talking about welding the doors shut again. For good."

"For good."

"For everybody's good."

"It doesn't have to be that way."

"I'm afraid it does." Just standing there, shaking his head as if any of this bothered him. "We'll have to put a great many things back in place. The militia, the drills, the alarm protocols and so forth."

"If you won't go," she said, "there's somebody else I've been working on."

"Weller."

"Weller."

"If he's leaving," Oates said, "tell him he should get out while the getting's good."

*

She didn't have to tell Weller. His mind was made up and he was itching to get under way, and so the next week became a period of the most intensive preparation he'd endured since the weeks he'd spent at Black Rose headquarters in Washington, studying tactics and survival under General Bainbridge.

Patel wrote everything out for him, formula after formula and procedure after procedure, but the truth was that she didn't really trust paper.

Paper could get lost. Paper could get ruined. Paper could be compromised or destroyed. So even though she wrote it all out she sat him down and taught it to him, line by line. Words and numbers and equations that meant nothing to Weller no matter how hard he tried. A labyrinth of signs and signifiers upon which everything depended. They spent the mornings that way, and in the afternoons he'd go out with Hutchinson and the kid to learn horsemanship. They had a perfectly good horse, after all, so why not make use of it.

Evenings he tried explaining himself to Liz again and again, reassuring her that one day he would return just as he'd returned before—only this time he'd come back with a cure for everything that ailed the world. All would be forgiven between him and Black Rose and AmeriBank, he was certain of that. Because what he was about to do would bring hope and security to everyone, Generic and Management and Ownership alike.

She didn't share his certainty. But she'd seen him before when he'd gotten this way, and she knew the impossibility of winning out over him in a test of wills.

He prepared himself to go, in other words, and she prepared herself to let him.

*

They resolved not to tell Penny until the last minute, rather than let the anticipation spoil this last certain week with her father. But they didn't need to tell her. That was clear when she awakened in the middle of the night, screaming into the darkness that her father was lost, lost, lost.

*

As for Oates, he spent the week in the Comm Center with a couple of his old lieutenants, getting the old gear dusted off and fired up.

Thirty-Two:

North

Penny stuck by him every single moment she was at home. She tried to talk her mother out of sending her to school, but in the end she went because her father told her she'd have spoiled his concentration in Dr. Patel's lab. What then? What if he got north and he'd lost the paperwork and he couldn't remember what he was supposed to remember because she'd been goofing around and distracting him? He convinced her that she was doing him a kindness by leaving him alone, even though it broke his heart to say so.

He found his old Black Rose compass in a drawer and he reminded her of how it worked and he let her choose where to put it in his pack. Someplace secure but handy, so he couldn't get lost. That was the word she'd woken up crying, wasn't it? *Lost?* She said it was, although maybe it didn't quite mean lost like *he'd lost his way.* Maybe it just meant lost. Gone.

Still, the compass helped and deciding where her father would keep it helped too. That was something. Something to hold onto.

*

As he left the car factory and heard the steel door close behind him, he cast a wary look toward the place near the treeline where Hutchinson had buried the horse. Meaning to keep his distance from it. Not knowing what kind of venomous infestation was swarming out there.

He headed north out of Spartanburg with the idea that it would take a couple of weeks, maybe three at the outside, to reach New York. He had food and water and a tent. He had a map, augmented by everything he'd learned on his last trip through the wilderness of the East. He also had a couple of pistols, along with plenty of ammunition. And in stark contrast to the pistols he had something else—a white cloth banner on a collapsible pole, which he was planning to wave at the first sign of anybody who looked like an authority figure. His plan was to throw himself upon the mercy of whoever showed up first, rather than brazen it out and risk making a target of himself. Reach for the sky and surrender. Explain the details later on.

He remembered as he rode off that the last time he'd left home he hadn't been alone. He'd had Penny with him, Penny holding his hand and Penny riding on his shoulders and Penny seeing everything there was to see for the very first time. Not clearly, of course. Not the way she would be able to see it now. That was the idea that kept him going as he moved northward. Through gray ruin gone emerald, he rode thinking that one day Penny would see the world he was seeing. It became his mission. To open the whole world up to his daughter. To free her of the bonds of Spartanburg and the threat of the virus. To set things right as he'd failed to set them right previously. To do it all for her, if for no one else.

Everyone everywhere would benefit from it sooner or later. He was confident of that if he was confident of anything. But it had to start with one person.

*

Some of the pages of the old Black Rose communications manual were stuck together, and a good deal of the ink had faded with the years, but it was still usable. More than usable. The maintenance section in the back was one big pulpy mass cemented together by moisture and eaten through by bugs, but the operating section in the front was just fine. All of the tables of codes and lists of frequencies were still legible, and that was everything Oates needed.

He pictured the satellites that his connection would depend on. There were still a couple over this part of the world that worked, he was fairly certain of that. Whether they'd communicate with the rest of the system well enough to make the connection was a question, but he had faith. And he had time, too, since Weller had two or three weeks of travel ahead of him.

*

Dr. Patel happened upon Oates coming out of the Comm Center, and seeing him there gave her an idea.

"I'd never really thought about it," she said, "but can we track Henry somehow? Keep an eye out? Watch his progress?"

Oates just shook his head. "I wish," he said.

"I wouldn't think we could *communicate* with him—"

"Hardly."

"But isn't there something?"

"Afraid not, Doc. Even if he had a brand in his neck, that'd be strictly local. A few feet at best. And it's not as if there are cameras out there."

"Not on the satellites?"

"You've been reading too much science fiction."

Dr. Patel nodded. "Sorry," she said. "It's just that you used to hear such outrageous stories. Black Rose surveillance and so forth."

"That's all they were, Doc. Stories. Even if they were true, I'd suspect the satellites would have deteriorated by now. Lost power and drifted out of alignment. And even if they were still working fine, I'm not exactly in the Black Rose loop anymore."

"Right," she said.

"I'm what you call *persona non grata.*"

"Of course you are. Of course. I was just thinking."

"Keep it up, Doc. Thinking's what we count on you for."

*

The compass was the compass, and north was north. The map, on the other hand, didn't exactly represent the world anymore. So much of everything was gone. You'd have to be an archaeologist to interpret what was left and align it with the orderly markings on a sheet of paper. It didn't matter much, though. He had the right general direction and he had plenty of supplies and he had the horse.

The horse made a huge difference. She was quieter than the old Harley he'd had his first trip down, and she was slower than the big sport utility he'd driven back, but all in all she set a rhythm and a pace that he found comforting. She was exactly the right scale for moving through these swamps and hills. Plus you could talk to her. Once each morning and once each afternoon he'd recite the formulas he'd learned from Patel, but the rest of the time he talked about Liz and Penny. Nonstop.

*

It was day three, and Oates was about halfway through the matrix of codes and frequencies when he hit pay dirt.

"It's Oates," he said into the mic as the static cleared. "That's right, Oates. Patch me over to General Bainbridge, pronto. You boys have incoming.".

Thirty-Three:

Inside

They met him dressed in Black Rose hazmat suits and armed with tear gas launchers, out beneath an overpass on the outskirts of that storied city of marble, White Washington. He raised his flag of surrender and climbed down off the horse and went quietly. Noticing that not a single member of the army around him carried an actual firearm. Noticing it but not thinking anything of it. They took him and they left the horse. Goodbye and good luck. He didn't have any say in the matter.

Washington seemed to be as close as they'd let him get to New York right now, and the truth was that they wouldn't even let him get as far as Washington. They loaded him into the back of a sealed transport and took a ramp up onto the highway, one of the old perimeter arteries that circled the city, and through a smeared and scratched portal of what was probably bullet-proof glass he watched as they eventually left that road and headed west. Away from the city. Another exit and they were on what must have once been a state road. It was rutted and strewn with rubble and he fastened himself down with a stray length of rope rather than be pitched around.

Nobody talked to him. Not before he got into the transport and not after they let him out. They just stood like mannequins come stiffly to life, pointing with their hands and with their tear gas launchers toward the closer of two enormous aircraft hangars. He tried stepping not toward the hangar but toward the men in the hazmat suits, putting an earnest expression on his face and lifting his hands skyward like some criminal caught in the act and turned contrite, but they just backed away and pointed all the more insistently.

He figured he could wait. These weren't the men he needed to negotiate with anyhow. He needed General Bainbridge. Somebody who called the shots and paid the bills.

They walked him to the hangar and inside through a double door, urging him on when he hesitated and directing him with small hand motions made clumsy by their oversized gear. He got the picture. Through a small entryway and then out into a gigantic atrium as big as the outdoors and crammed full of airplanes. Airplanes on the ground and airplanes hanging from the ceiling. Little antique biplanes and powerful battle-scarred fighters and outlandishly shaped monstrosities that had gone into outer space and come back. A museum of flight.

They gave him no time to marvel at it. Instead they urged him down a long central corridor and through an unprepossessing steel door and into a warren of office and storage spaces. The hallway lit by dim bulbs in dusty iron cages hung from the ceiling. Weller thinking they were taking him to somebody with authority, but reconsidering when he noticed that some of the doors they were passing now had heavy bolts and padlocks and hinged slits at waist level. At the end of the hall, beneath the last of the caged bulbs, stood a door that had been modified. Plastic sheeting hung in strips over it, and the edges had been sealed with rubber stripping. The hinged slit likewise. Only the heavy bolt and the padlock were unchanged.

This was where they were taking him. They'd improved it on his behalf and their own. Isolation.

*

Behind his desk at the Pentagon, General Bainbridge got the word. *The cat's in the cradle. The eagle has landed.* Some coded nonsense on that order. *Mission accomplished* at any rate. Now he had a decision to make. Two customers and anybody's guess which of them would turn out to be the more profitable. He had a bottom line to worry about, after all.

He figured PharmAgra had suffered the greater losses. All those good working people killed in the firestorm in Connecticut. Working people and customers both. There was no telling how much economic pain PharmA-gra had endured as a result, insurance or no insurance, and there was no guessing how much punishment they'd want to heap on the individual re-sponsible. He knew the head of the operation, a certain Marie DuPont, but he didn't know her well. A bean-counter and a data-head. Child of Ameri-can royalty, her life devoted to adding up the numbers at the end of the line. She'd know right down to the penny how much Weller's shenanigans had cost. He could only wonder how much revenge would be worth.

AmeriBank, on the other hand, had Anderson Carmichael. The richest man in the world and one of the least principled. He'd been cheated out of that little girl's operation and he'd had his precious car stolen and wrecked, all because he'd been trying to keep his word to a lowdown unscrupulous Generic. Or at least he'd see it that way, and that's all that counted. Weller would be worth a pile of AmeriBank scrip to Carmichael. How big a pile, exactly? That would depend on how hot he still was. How much he still wanted that car he'd been unable to get. And how wronged he still felt.

*

The men in the hazmat suits indicated that Weller should leave everything in the hallway. His pack. His clothing. Everything. They showed him a plastic sack to put everything in, and another plastic sack to put the first sack inside. They had him seal it up with a cable tie, and then they sent him into the cell and threw the bolt behind him and locked the door. Wel-ler put his ear to the cold steel and didn't hear anything, not even retreating footsteps, until a hissing sound started up. A piercing smell of chemicals leaked in through the rubberized slit. Some kind of decontamination proc-ess out in hall. He guessed they figured they were safe now.

If they'd just given him an ear, they'd have known that already. But so what. You couldn't blame them for being cautious.

The room had a cot and a chair and a chemical toilet. A camera and a microphone and a speaker mounted high up near the ceiling in the farthest corner where he wasn't supposed to notice them. Some old cabinets and counters and drawers built in and emptied out but not entirely. One of the drawers had a burned-out light bulb in it and another one had a couple of old copper pennies that were probably worth something. He didn't have a pocket to put them in so he just let them stay.

He sat on the bed for a while and used the chemical toilet and looked around in the rest of the drawers just for something to kill time. Finding dust and paper clips and the sorry stub of a pencil.

*

"It's only a precaution," said Oates. "We'll just weld these doors shut until Henry returns. There's that dead horse out there, don't forget. It's not that far away. Anything could get into it. A bird, for heaven's sake. Just an innocent bird. Which reminds me, we'd better seal off those high windows too. Just to make certain. Just until Henry comes back with the cure."

*

It occurred to Weller that Patel had been right. She'd been concerned that the paper she'd written out might go missing somewhere along the way, and now it had. The men in the hazmat suits had taken it along with everything else, and it had probably been incinerated already. But now he had a pencil. And he still had everything she'd put into his head. So he picked out an empty spot on one of the plain white walls, and he began to write it all out.

His concentration was so complete that he didn't even notice when the red light on the camera in the far corner began to blink.

*

Bainbridge hadn't run the Joint Chiefs under President Cheney for no reason. And by God he hadn't spent time in that position without learning a lesson or two from the Angler himself, the resurrected and semi-robotic Final President of The United States of America.

He decided on a conference call. He'd talk to DuPont at PharmAgra and Carmichael at AmeriBank together. Give them both the good news at the same time. They'd know what he was up to—they'd smell a bidding war right off—but so be it. It would clear the decks. It would let everybody get right down to business.

His lieutenants wrangled with their gatekeepers for a few minutes before everything was set up, during which time Bainbridge watched Weller through the camera. He was writing something on the walls of his cell. Letters and numbers and symbols that meant nothing to Bainbridge. It looked like writing made by some kind of aliens from outer space. An unknown language, spelling out a message or a memorial. Who could tell what it was? Who cared?

Weller didn't look sick, though. That was one thing. He didn't seem to be weak and he wasn't bleeding anywhere. They'd give him a couple of weeks in isolation to make sure, and at the same time they'd go through his belongings with a microscope. If he didn't have the virus in his blood, he must have it stowed with his gear. They'd find it. They'd find it for sure. And even if they didn't, there'd be a report that said they did. *All the better to eat you with, my dear.*

DuPont and Carmichael showed up in split-screen at the same instant. She looked annoyed and he looked disgusted. He just grinned at them and began.

"We've been pursuing a certain friend of yours for a while now," he said, "and he's finally come to light."

"Weller," said Carmichael.

"Exactly."

DuPont looked interested all of a sudden. She'd been holding a sheet of paper in one hand, and she put it aside.

Carmichael leaned in. "Where is he?"

"In our custody. Isolated. Don't worry about that."

"Why would I worry about that?"

"Because he's carrying the virus," said Bainbridge. "We had it on good authority that he'd weaponized himself and set out for New York. Luckily for you folks, we were able to apprehend him in time."

"Prove you've got him," said DuPont.

Click.

And there he was on the screen. He had his back to the camera but there was no question of his identity. Not in Carmichael's mind anyhow.

He'd been dreaming of him for a long time now. Dreaming of this moment. The way he jumped at the sight of the naked figure penciling his testimony on the wall was enough to convince DuPont as well.

"What's he writing?" Carmichael asked.

"I have no idea. A message of some sort. Something he wants to communicate. God knows. Maybe the virus has gone to his head."

DuPont disagreed. "It doesn't work that way."

"Of all people," said Bainbridge, "you'd be the one to know."

"I would. I'd bet he's clean."

"Could be," said Bainbridge. "We'll know soon enough. But whatever he's up to, it's time we talked business."

She raised a finger. "Can I bring someone else in, just for another pair of eyes?"

That was fine with Bainbridge. She didn't have the deep personal pockets that Carmichael did. She'd need approval for the kind of expenditure they'd be talking about any minute now.

She pressed a buzzer and whispered something into a secondary mic and they all waited until another figure appeared behind her. A squat figure in a lab coat. He studied the screen for a few seconds, and then he vanished just like that.

"Very well," she said when he was gone. "Let's talk."

*

"Yes, ma'am," said the squat man in the lab coat. He was holding a magnified screen dump from the conference call, running his finger along the lines that Weller had written on the wall of his cell. "If this isn't a cure for the virus, it's darned close."

"How long until you can synthesize it?"

"A week, maybe two. But there'll have to be some extended testing to follow. And I do mean extended."

"What if we had someone who was infected?" she said. "Someone you could test it on? An active case?"

"That's not likely," said the man in the lab coat.

"Oh, I think I could make it happen," said Marie Dupont. And she smiled as she reached for the telephone.

About the Author

Sam Winston is the pen name of Jon Clinch, prizewinning author of *Finn, Kings of the Earth,* and *The Thief of Auschwitz.*

Web site: jonclinch.com
Twitter: @jonclinch
Facebook: facebook.com/JonClinchBooks